emma
all Stirred Up

First published in Great Britain in 2013 by
Simon and Schuster UK Ltd
A CBS COMPANY

Originally published in the USA in 2012 by Simon Spotlight,
an imprint of Simon & Schuster Children's Division, New York.

Copyright © 2012 by Simon and Schuster, Inc. Text by Tracey West.
Design by Laura Roode.

Simon & Schuster UK Ltd
1st Floor,
222 Gray's Inn Road,
London
WC1X 8HB

Simon & Schuster Australia, Sydney
Simon & Schuster India, New Delhi

This book is a work of fiction. Names, characters, places and incidents
are either the product of the author's imagination or are used fictitiously.
Any resemblance to actual people living or dead,
events or locales is entirely coincidental.

A CIP catalogue record for this book is available from the British Library.

ISBN 978-1-4711-1554-7

1 3 5 7 9 10 8 6 4 2

Printed and bound in Great Britain.

www.simonandschuster.co.uk
www.simonandschuster.com.au

The
Cupcake Diaries

Emma
all
Stirred Up

Coco Simon

SIMON AND SCHUSTER

CHAPTER 1

Little Brother, Big Problem

$\mathcal{M}$y name is Emma Taylor, but a few weeks ago I was wishing it was anything but! I was pretending that the little boy who was outside the school bus, wailing that he did not want to go to day camp, was *not* my little brother, Jake Taylor, and that those desperate parents who were bribing and pleading with him were *not* my parents, but rather some poor, misguided souls whom I would never see again.

In fact, I was wishing that I was already an adult and that my three best friends and I — the entire Cupcake Club — had opened our own bakery on a cute little side street in New York City, where none of my three brothers lived. The bakery would be all pink, and it would sell piles of cupcakes in a rainbow of lovely colours and flavours, and would cater mainly to movie stars and little girls' princess birthday parties. That is my fantasy. Sounds great, right?

But oh, no, this was reality.

"Emmy!" Jake was shrieking as my father gently but firmly manhandled him down the bus aisle to where I was scrunched down on my seat, pretending not to see them. I could literally feel the warmth of all the other eyes on the bus watching us, and I just wanted to melt away. Instead I stared out the window, like there was something really fascinating out there.

"Emma, please look after your brother," said my father. How many times have I heard that one? My older brothers, Matt and Sam, and I take turns babysitting Jake, but somehow the bad stuff always happens on my shift. My dad gave Jake one last kiss, reached to pat me on the head and then dashed off the bus. I wished I could've dashed with him.

A counsellor sat on the end of the seat, scrunching Jake in between us, so he couldn't run away. Jake was wailing, and the counsellor – a nice girl named Paige, who is about twenty-one years old and probably wishing she were somewhere else too – was speaking in a soothing voice to him. She looked over his head at me, smiled, and then said, "Don't worry. This happens all the time. We always

2

get one of these guys. He'll settle down within the week."

The week?! I wanted to die, but instead I nodded and looked out the window again. I also wanted to kill Jake that moment, but it was only seconds later that his wails turned to quiet hiccups. Then he slid his clammy, chubby little hand into mine and squeezed, and I felt a little guilty. "It's going to be okay, Jake," I whispered, and squeezed his little hand back. He snuggled into me and looked up at me with these really big eyes that get me every time. It's not the worst thing in the world to have a little someone in your life who looks up to you.

I sighed. "Feeling better, officer?" Jake is big into law enforcement, so it usually cheers him up if we play Policeman. At least he wasn't crying anymore. Paige gave him a pat on the head and then went to help some other kids get on the bus. But Jake wasn't feeling better. I could tell just by looking at him.

"I feel sick," he said.

Oh no. Jake isn't one of those kids who fakes being sick. My mum always says on car trips that if Jake says he feels sick, we pull over, because he *will* throw up, 100 percent of the time.

I jerked the bus window open and quickly flung

Jake over me, so that he was sitting in the window seat. "Put your head out the window, buddy. Take deep breaths – in through your nose, out through your mouth. We're going to start moving soon, so the wind will be in your face. . . Deep breaths."

I rubbed his back a little and looked up to see if anyone I knew was getting on at this stop. My best friend and co–Cupcake Clubber Alexis Becker was going to the same camp, but her parents were dropping her off on their way to work. I fantasised about them driving me, too, and leaving Jake to his own devices. Ha! As if my parents would let me get away with that! At the very least, I did have our Cupcake Club meeting to look forward to later today. Just quality girl time, planning out the club's summer schedule and reviewing the cupcake jobs we had coming up. Chilling with my best friends – Alexis, Katie and Mia – and brainstorming. It was definitely going to be fun.

A bunch of little kids streamed on and sat mostly in the front of the bus. Suddenly I spied a familiar shade of very bright blonde hair, and my stomach sank. Noooo!!! It couldn't be.

But it was.

Sydney Whitman, mean-girl extraordinaire and head of the imaginatively named Popular Girls

Club at school, came strolling down the aisle, heading straight for the back row, where only the most popular kids dared to sit. I quickly looked out the window and pretended I hadn't seen her. But no luck.

"Oh, that's so cute! You and your little brother sitting together! I guess that's easier than trying to find someone your own age to sit with?" She smiled sweetly, but her remark stung just as it was meant to.

Jake hates Sydney as much as I do, if not more, so when he turned his head to look at her, he began to gag. Sydney's eyes opened wide, and her hand flew up to cover her mouth. "Oh no! He's going to—"

Luckily, Jake turned to the window just in time and hurled the contents of his stomach out onto the road.

"Disgusting!" shrieked Sydney, and she fled to the back of the bus.

I didn't know whether to laugh or cry. It's just one more nail in the coffin of my possible popularity, not that I ever really stood a chance. And not that I really wanted to. But it was also kind of hilarious to have Jake take one look at Sydney and then throw up. Definitely not her desired effect on men. I made a mental note to tell the Cupcake Club later. They'd love this.

Jake barfed a couple more times and then sat back down, looking as white as a sheet. The good news about Jake's car sickness is that after he's done throwing up, he's always fine. I pulled a napkin from my lunch bag and gave it to him to wipe his face. Then I cracked open his thermos and gave him a tiny sip of apple juice. I felt sorry for the poor guy. I hate throwing up.

Jake smiled wanly. "Thanks, Emmy. Sorry."

I laughed. "I feel the same way when I see Sydney Whitman." I wasn't sure I would have been so psyched about going to this camp if I'd known Sydney was going – or at the very least that she'd be on my bus. It definitely put a cramp in my happiness.

Jake rested his head back against the seat and promptly fell asleep. In a minute his head was resting, sweaty and heavy, against my shoulder. First days can be hard for anyone, especially little kids. At least tomorrow we wouldn't have the same problem. I said a silent prayer that Sydney wasn't in my group.

At camp, we got off the bus and a crowd of cheering counsellors with painted faces was there to greet us. My mum must've called ahead to tip off someone, because one really pretty counsellor was holding up a sign, like people do at the airport. It read OFFICER JAKE TAYLOR. That at least allowed me to peel him off and hand him over to the counsellor, so I could go with my group, Team Four, to our rally zone (whatever that was) at the arts-and-crafts centre.

The boys and girls have separate areas at camp, so I wouldn't see Jake again all day, thank goodness. And thank goodness again, because Sydney headed off with Team Five in the opposite direction. I didn't have a minute to review who was on whose team. Anyway, I didn't know a lot of the kids, but I did know that wherever Alexis was, she and I would be together. (We requested it, and my mum promised me she had spoken with the camp director.) That's all that matters.

As I headed across the green lawn to the arts-and-crafts centre, I heard someone calling my name. I turned, and, of course, it was Alexis! I had never been so happy to see her in all my life.

"Thank goodness!" I cried, and threw my arms around her, like a shipwreck victim who has finally been saved.

Alexis isn't much for big displays of affection, so she patted my back awkwardly, but I didn't mind. In any case, she just saw me a few days ago.

"What's going on?" she asked as we separated and followed our counsellor.

"Jake drama. Screaming, puking – the whole deal." I lowered my voice. "And Sydney Whitman saw the whole thing."

Alexis waved her hand in the air, as if to say *whatever!* That is just one of the many things I love about Alexis. She doesn't care at all what other people think. "Too bad he didn't puke *on* her," she said with a laugh. "Or did he?" Her eyes twinkled mischievously.

"No such luck. But the good news is, we aren't on the same team as her."

We'd reached the log cabin that was the headquarters for our team. On its porch stood two teenage counsellors – a guy and a girl. As the crowd amassed in front of them, I counted twelve campers: all girls, of course. Yay! Finally! A break from all the boys in my life!

"Hello, people! Listen up!" The guy counsellor was clapping his hands and kind of dancing around in a funny way to get our attention. Everyone started laughing and listening.

He bowed and said, "Thank you, ladies! My name is Raoul Sanchez, and this is my awesome partner, Maryanne Murphy."

8

Maryanne did a little curtsy, and we all clapped. She was pretty – short and cute with red hair and freckles. Raoul was tall and thin with rubbery arms and legs, and his face had a big goofy smile topped off by black, crew-cut hair. It was obvious neither of them was shy.

"We are going to have the most fun of any team this summer! Raoul and I personally guarantee it!" Maryanne said enthusiastically.

Raoul nodded. "If this isn't the most fun summer of your life, when camp is over I will take you to an all-you-can-eat pizza party, on me."

There were cheers and claps.

"Okay, we have a lot to tell you, so why don't you all grab a seat on the grass and get ready to be pumped!" said Maryanne.

Raoul and Maryanne then proceeded to tell us how we'd get to pick our own team name. ("Team Four" was just a placeholder, they said.) They told us about all the fun activities we'd do: swimming, kayaking, art projects, team sports, field trips, tennis and more. Then they told us about the special occasions that were scheduled: Tie-Dye Day, Pyjama Day, Costume Day, Crazy Hat Day and finally, the best day of all . . . Camp Olympics, followed by the grand finale: the camp talent show!

Ugh. The camp talent show? Getting onstage in front of more than a hundred people? *So* not up my alley. I made a face at Alexis, but she was listening thoughtfully, her head tilted to the side and her long reddish hair already escaping its headband. She was probably wondering if there was any money to be made here; business was mostly all she thought about. In fact, her parents said if she did an outdoor camp for part of the summer, she could go to business camp for two weeks at the end of the summer. Sometimes I wonder how we are friends at all; our interests are so different!

"Thinking of signing up?" I whispered.

"Myself? No. But you should," she whispered back.

I laughed. "Yeah, right. What's my talent? Babysitting?"

Alexis raised her eyebrows at me. "Maybe. But I'm sure you can come up with something more marketable than that."

Right. I can't even keep the kid I babysit for from throwing up.

CHAPTER 2

Meet the Hotcakes!

First we played a getting-to-know-you game called Pass the Packet. We had a mystery brown bag filled with something, and we each took turns holding it and telling the group about ourselves and then said what we wished was in the bag. (I told the group I had three brothers and I wished the bag had tickets to a taping of *Top Chef*.) When it was Alexis's turn, she told the group how she, Mia, Katie and I had a Cupcake Club and about all the business we do, baking cupcakes for special events. The other girls in the group thought it was so cool. I felt great, and Alexis and I promised to bring in cupcakes for the group.

At the end, Maryanne opened the "packet," and it was filled with these awesome friendship bracelets for each of us. We all grabbed for the colour we wanted. I, of course, grabbed a pink one.

Then we got down to business, naming our team.

A very pretty girl named Georgia, with light red hair and dark eyes, suggested we be "Rock Stars." I thought it was a great idea, but because it was the first idea, everyone still wanted a chance to make their own suggestions.

A girl named Caroline, who turned out to be Georgia's cousin, said, "How about the 'A-Team,'" which everyone thought was funny. Alexis suggested "Winners," because the power of positive branding would intimidate our competitors. I had to laugh. Then a girl named Charlotte – with bright blue eyes and dark, dark hair – suggested that since we would be having cupcakes a lot (she laughed and looked at me and Alexis when she said it), we should be the "Cupcakes." Right after she said it, a funny girl named Elle said, "No, the 'Hotcakes'!" and that was it.

"The Hotcakes! I love it!" cried Raoul. He and Elle high-fived. "Let's take a vote, girls! All in favour of the 'Hotcakes,' put your hands in the air!"

Everyone screamed and waved their hands high,

and that was that. Maryanne announced it was time for the Hotcakes to change for swimming, then lunchtime.

Alexis and I grabbed our backpacks and headed to the changing rooms.

"This is superfun, don't you think?" I asked as we walked across the central green.

"Yes, *and* I think we have the best group," said Alexis in a sure voice.

I laughed. "How do you know?"

She shrugged. "I counted how many girls we have versus the other two teams in our age group, then I evaluated how many of our girls are nice and smart. As a percentage, we have the nicest team by far. I would also venture that one hundred percent of our team is smart, and with Sydney on Team Five and stupid Bella on Team Three, their intelligence rate is at least ten percent below ours."

"Alexis! You are too much!" I shook my head. "The only bad part is, I wish the others were here."

She knew who I meant. Katie and Mia from our Cupcake Club were doing different things from us this month. Alexis frowned thoughtfully. "Yeah. But we'll see them plenty. And maybe it's good for us to branch out a little. It will generate some new business strategies and connections!"

I swatted her. "Is that all you think about?"

She pushed open the door to the locker room with a grin. "Pretty much!"

"I just hope they don't replace us with new friends."

Alexis shrugged. "Maybe they're thinking the same thing."

I thought back to last autumn, when Katie had been dumped by Callie, her old best friend, so that Callie could hang with Sydney and the Popular Girls Club. New friends and old: a tough thing to balance. I sighed after just thinking about it.

When I came to the open house they had in March, one of the things I liked about this camp was that they have private changing rooms in the locker room, so you don't have to strip naked in front of strangers. I could never change in front of other people. Forget about being naked and getting into a swimming costume – I can't even change into pj's at a slumber party or try on clothes at the shops if someone else is in the room. Except for Mum. It's just a personal thing. I am very private about my body. Maybe it comes from being the only girl in a family of boys or from having my own room, but I just like privacy.

Alexis and I changed in rooms next to each other, and were chatting through the opening at the top of the dividers.

"Wait till you see my new suit!" she said. "It's so cute!"

"Me too! My mum brought it home as a surprise!"

We came out and took one look at each other and then started laughing our heads off. We had on the exact same swimming costume! They were tankinis, navy blue with white piping and a cool, yellow lightning bolt down either side. Alexis is kind of muscular from soccer, and I'm kind of thin (I play the flute, but that doesn't exactly build muscles!), so the suit fit us way differently. We couldn't stop giggling, though. We looked like total dork twins.

Georgia and Elle, and Charlotte and Caroline all gathered around, and we admired what everyone was wearing. We all had on new suits. Then one girl named Kira, who was shy and superpretty, came out. She had her towel draped around her shoulders, and she wasn't smiling.

"Let's see!" said Elle, clapping.

Kira shook her head. "Uh-uh." She bit her lip, and we instantly realised we shouldn't push her.

She looked like she might cry at any second.

"Okay!" Alexis said quickly. I could tell she was desperate to make Kira feel better, but couldn't think of how. Suddenly she hoisted her towel across her shoulders, to cover herself like Kira. "Capes it is!" I was so proud of her right then for her idea.

Everyone followed suit. Georgia yelled, "The Hot*capes*!" and we all hooted. I glanced at Kira and saw relief on her face, and we all marched out to meet Maryanne and Raoul, who were waiting outside to walk us to the huge pool. I had to wonder how bad Kira's suit was, though.

We sat for a water safety lecture by the lifeguard and swim director, Mr Collins, a really nice P.E. teacher from the primary school whom I recognised. The safety talk was a little boring (yeah, yeah, don't run, no chicken fights, no diving in the shallow end, swim with a buddy), but then we were in the water for free swim, and it was heavenly! The water wasn't too cold and the pool was huge, with a supershallow end and a superdeep end with a diving board!

In my excitement to get in the water, I had forgotten to check out Kira's suit, but I stole a glance the first chance I could. She was kind of cringing in the shallow end, and her suit was a one piece with Hello Kitty on it, and it was way too small for her. I felt terrible. It was babyish and it looked bad. I wondered why she didn't just swim to the deep end to cover it up.

"Okay, people! Now it's time for some fun!" Mr Collins blew a whistle and beckoned us all over to the wall in the shallow end. I love to swim and I'm pretty good at it, so I did a loopy backstroke, kind of hamming it up, and Alexis did her old lady breaststroke, where she keeps her head out of the water the whole time. We cracked each other up.

Once everyone had reached the side of the pool, Mr Collins whistled again to get our attention, then he spoke. He had a very kind voice, and was very quiet and patient.

"Okay, kids, today we're going to just get a feel for skill level and what we need to work on with each of you. One of the great things about Spring Lake Day Camp is that you will all leave here swimming really well by the end of the summer, and you'll have fun learning! So let's break you into four groups of three, and we'll have each of you swim a length of the pool in three heats. Count off by threes, then come down to the shallow end and we'll get started."

17

Alexis and I swam stood next to each other in the lineup, so we would be on the same team. I was first, and Charlotte was the third in our group. The other girls arranged themselves, and Maryanne and Raoul followed, walking along the edge of the pool. The counsellors were in swimming costumes, but I guess they didn't have to get in the water since Mr Collins taught this part of camp.

"Okay, girls. Everyone settled? Any stroke you like, no rush. We're not racing. On your marks, get set ... *bweeet!*" He blew his whistle hard, and I took off, swimming freestyle, all the way to the deep end. I knew we weren't racing, but it felt good to try hard and swim fast. I hated knowing people were watching me, but at least three other girls were swimming at the same time as me, so the bystanders weren't watching *only* me the whole time, which made it okay.

I got to the deep end and slapped my hand against the wall. First! (Not that we were racing!) I hung on to the wall and watched Georgia, Jesse, and Caroline come in right after me. I was breathing hard, but it felt good. Next up was Alexis, along with a girl named Tricia, a girl named Louise and Kira in the fourth group. Mr Collins blew the whistle, and they were off.

Alexis is a great swimmer too. Just what you would expect: efficient; not show-offy; fast, clean strokes. Tricia and Louise were doing fine too. But . . . uh-oh. Kira wasn't.

She had pushed away from the wall fine and was gliding, but then when the water got deeper and her glide wore off, she started to flounder. She put down her feet and tried to push off again, but that only got her into the deeper end, to where she couldn't stand. She started to sink.

Mr Collins was in the water in a flash, as was Raoul. They both dove from opposite sides of the water and reached her at the exact same moment. I was frozen to the spot, watching as they grabbed her and hauled her towards the side of the pool. *Oh my goodness,* was all I could think. Kira can't swim!

When they reached the wall, Kira was sputtering and coughing. They each had an arm around her, and had towed her to the side in a flash. Mr Collins lifted her onto the deck and pushed himself up and out of the water. Maryanne came running over with her own towel, and put it over Kira's shoulders. Kira started to cry. Tricia, Alexis and Louise had reached the deep end's wall (they'd been oblivious to what had happened), and now everyone was just silent, watching.

At first, we were all scared for Kira, and then as it became clear that she was okay, we were all really embarrassed for her.

Mr Collins quickly established that Kira was not hurt or in danger, then stood and called out to the group, "She's fine! Just a little rusty, like the best of us after a long winter! Everything's okay. Just swim for a minute while we change our plan." He and Maryanne and Raoul chatted in whispers, then Raoul jumped back into the pool and swam to the shallow end.

Mr Collins called out again, "Now is there anyone else who'd like a little extra practise with Raoul? It's fine! Just raise your hand." He looked around. No one was raising their hand. But then Elle, who was still in the shallow end, raised her hand.

"Great! Go with Raoul to the corner and you'll work on it a little. Kira"—Mr Collins reached down and patted Kira's head—"just come on over and join Raoul and . . . what's your name, young lady?"

"Elle," called Elle.

"And Elle while they practise at this end, okay? The next group, get ready to swim."

In a few moments Kira was back in the water

with Elle and Raoul. Now, if there is one thing I noticed when we were having free swim, it's that Elle is an amazing swimmer. After what she did for Kira, I knew she'd make an amazing friend, too.

CHAPTER 3

New Friends, Old Friends and Old Enemies

Sydney Whitman sat at a picnic table next to us at lunch. She must've been bragging to her group that she knew a lot of kids at camp, because she had walked right over to us and acted really chummy. (She was obviously going for quantity over quality since we're not friends.) We weren't falling for it, though, and anyone could see she was really just doing it for show.

"What, no cupcakes?" Sydney asked, with a big fake smile as she inspected our lunch.

Alexis shook her head. "Nope." She continued eating, as though Sydney wasn't even there. The rest of our table (Charlotte, Elle, Georgia and Kira – Elle's new best friend) just looked blankly at Sydney, probably wondering who she was.

Sydney was floundering. She tried a different topic. "So what's your team name, girls?"

Georgia, who was so sweet, was perplexed. She clearly felt uncomfortable with Alexis's rudeness, while I for one was loving it.

"We're called the Hotcakes," Georgia said politely.

Sydney laughed meanly, but she had a kind of surprised look on her face. "That's so . . . like, young. Like Strawberry Shortcake or something. We're Angels, like *Charlie's Angels*. Gorgeous and powerful, get it?" She flipped her hair.

Georgia and Elle looked at each other, then at me, like *Who is this person?* I just had to shrug.

"I heard someone in your group almost drowned today," Sydney said next, really casually.

I looked at Kira and saw her face turn a deep red. I wanted to throttle Sydney. Instead, I thought about what Elle did earlier and how brave and kind she was. I decided to copy her.

"It was me." I shrugged.

Sydney's hand flew to her mouth, and she started to laugh in surprise. "Really! You can't swim?"

"Actually, it was me," said Alexis.

Sydney looked confused. "Wait, what?"

Georgia was laughing now. "It was me. I fell into the pool and drowned."

"No, me!" said Elle. Now we were all howling. Even Kira was giggling a little.

Sydney looked at us, one to another, then she got a mad look on her face and gave a slight shrug. "Whatever. I'm just trying to be a concerned citizen." And she stalked back to her table. That last line really got us going. While I know it isn't nice to laugh at other people, it felt good to be part of this group and laughing for a good reason. The very idea of Sydney Whitman as a caring, concerned individual was truly hilarious to me. Of course, when we stopped laughing, Alexis and I explained who she was and why she was such a villain. There's nothing like a common enemy to unite a group. That's when Alexis spontaneously promised to start cupcake Fridays for camp, and I wholeheartedly agreed.

The first day of camp seemed to last forever. It was only four o'clock when we all piled back onto the bus, but it seemed like I'd left home weeks, not hours, earlier.

Jake was sticky and muddy and tired when I met him at our bus waiting area. He promptly handed me his grimy, mud-caked towel and wet backpack to hold for him, thereby killing my happy first-day-of-camp glow. At least Alexis was on the bus ride home with me. But as it turned out, Jake wouldn't let her sit with us. He pitched a fit that he wanted to sit with only me, so Alexis sat in front of me so we could chat on the way home. And after all that, Jake fell asleep as soon as the wheels started turning. Apparently he only pukes on the way *to* camp.

Alexis and I spoke in whispers as we reviewed the day, kind of free-associating.

Me: "Mr Collins is really nice."

Alexis: "Yeah, that was scary."

Me: "Very cool of Elle to pretend she needed help."

Alexis: "I'm psyched for cupcake Fridays at camp, too."

Me: "I wish SW wasn't here."

Alexis: *(Moans. Pretends to puke.)*

We laughed.

But then Alexis grew serious. "You know, I learned more about Kira, because Louisa went to school with her. I feel really bad. Her mum was sick for a few years, and she died about eight months ago. Kira has three much older sisters, but none of them live at home anymore, so she just lives with her dad. He's, like, much older than our dads and kind of clueless and sad about his wife and everything."

"Wow. That is so sad. Poor Kira."

Alexis nodded. "I know. So that kind of explains the lame swimming costume. I guess her dad didn't know which kind to buy her. And maybe her mum just wasn't well enough to teach her to swim, and maybe her dad didn't know you had to know how to swim to go to this camp."

"Bummer. I felt terrible for her."

"Yeah, but at least she's really nice," said Alexis.

"And superpretty," I added, feeling generous. I made a mental note to make an even bigger effort with Kira. Even though my mum isn't around a lot, it would be really hard if she was gone for, like, forever. I couldn't even imagine it.

We had reached Alexis's stop, so she hopped off. We were having a Cupcake Club meeting at her house at five thirty, but I was going to go home and shower first. I'd see her again soon.

Just before our stop, I nudged Jake awake, and when we arrived, I half carried, half dragged him and his disgusting gear off the bus. He was so dirty, I considered hosing him down in the yard, but instead I talked him into a bath by promising him that he could use one of the fizzy blue bath bombs I got for my birthday. His gear I would have to hose off.

I spent a lot of time babysitting Jake earlier in the year, when my mum had to switch jobs for a little while. It was hard work and kind of a bummer because Jake is not the easiest kid to babysit. Also, it cut into a lot of my own activities. Now that my mum is back at her old job, things are a little better. During the summer, I have to take Jake to and from camp, and two days a week I stay with him until 5:15 p.m., when my mum gets home. The other days my older brothers, Matt and Sam, take turns watching him.

After Jake's bath, I got him into his pj's and settled him in front of the TV, and then I showered and cleared out my lunchbox and backpack. At 5:10 I was ready. At 5:20 my mum had not yet appeared. At 5:30 I called Alexis's house to say my mum was running late. At 5:40 she pulled in. I was waiting in the driveway with my arms folded and my bike all ready to go.

"Honey, I'm so sorry," my mum said as she clambered out of the car with all her shopping bags. "The checkout line was horrible, and it took longer than

I'd planned, plus, they were out of the good tortillas for the quesadillas Dad likes, so . . ."

My blood was boiling. I was all ready to start yelling at her about how I'm always left stranded, always ditched with Jake; how no one ever considers my schedule, and so on. But suddenly I thought of Kira and how hard it must have been for her to lose her mum. I took a deep breath; kissed my mum on the cheek; yelled, "See you later!"; and took off.

I was twenty minutes late for the meeting. I needed to be home by six thirty for dinner, so that only gave us forty minutes to meet.

"Mia! Katie! You are a sight for sore eyes!" I said, and it was true. Because even though I saw them yesterday, it felt like a year ago. And it was so exhausting trying to make new friends that it was a great relief to relax with old ones. I just sat and smiled at them like an idiot for a minute.

"Ookaaay . . ." said Katie, and giggled. "We missed you, too."

Alexis had filled them in on camp, but then I had to give my version and they had to tell me about their day. So it was 6:10 by the time we finished, and we only had ten minutes for club business — fifteen minutes if I biked home really fast.

28

"First order," said Alexis in her official voice. "I need someone to take over my deliveries to Mona on Saturdays. I now have a summer golf clinic on Saturday mornings."

Every Friday we bake five dozen mini cupcakes for our friend Mona, who owns a bridal store called The Special Day. We met her when Mia's mum got married and we were all bridesmaids in the wedding. We bought our dresses at Mona's store. The store is so beautiful and peaceful and girlie (so unlike my house!), and Mona is so nice. I waved my hand in the air.

"I'll take over!" I said. "I will, I will!"

Everyone laughed.

Alexis beamed. "Great. Thanks. Next, Jake's birthday."

I groaned. "What colour cupcake would 'annoying' be?"

Mia loves Jake (it's mutual), so she protested. "No, they have to be really special. Our best work for that little mascot of ours!"

Katie asked, "What about P–B–and–J?"

"Nah, peanut allergies in his class," I said.

"Triple Chocolate Fudge Explosion?" suggested Katie.

"Why don't we just ask him?" asked Mia.

"Fine." I wrote it on my to-do list. (I am all about lists.)

"What else?" asked Alexis.

"Well, I was wondering if we should try to mix things up a little for Mona. Maybe try a different flavour?" asked Katie.

"Yes, but it has to be white," reminded Mia. Right now we baked only white cake cupcakes with white frosting because Mona can't have anything chocolate or, like, raspberry in a store full of white, white, white bridal gowns!

We thought for a minute.

"Cinnamon bun with cream cheese frosting?" I suggested.

"Ooh, I love those!" said Mia enthusiastically.

"Or coconut?" suggested Katie.

Alexis made a face. "Not everyone likes coconut," she said.

"Also maybe allergies, right?" I said.

Katie looked kind of bummed, so I said, "Why don't I ask her on Saturday, okay?"

Alexis made a note in the meeting minutes, and I added it to my to-do list. Sometimes being in this club is about balancing people's feelings as much as it is about baking and making money. It can be hard work.

"So Friday night, we're on, right? My house?" I said.

Alexis and Mia nodded eagerly. They have crushes on my older brothers (Alexis on Matt, Mia on Sam), so they always want to come to my house. And ever since I bought my own pink KitchenAid stand mixer, it's gotten much more efficient to bake at my house too.

I wondered if Alexis and I should mention that we're baking for our new friends on Thursday, too. I glanced at Alexis to see if she was thinking about it, but her face betrayed nothing. I decided to wait.

It's weird having other friends. I wondered if they'd become as close as my old friends. I really couldn't picture it!

divine

CHAPTER 4

A Secret Celebrity!

So, when I thought Jake's crying and barfing were just first-day jitters I was dead wrong! They were *every day* jitters! My mornings were exhausting and mortifying. Seriously, every morning he got himself all worked up, he cried, Dad made me sit with him, and then he puked. It was completely, totally unfair.

I tried to go on strike and get a ride with Alexis, but my parents insisted I take the bus so that I could watch over Jake. The only good thing was that because I did bus duty (and maybe because instead of freaking out at my mum when she was late that time from picking up shopping, I was nice!), my parents declared that I didn't have to babysit Jake anymore when we got home! Now it was all up to

Matt and Sam (and my mum). Yay! Freedom!

Needless to say, the bus was still a major bummer. And Sydney made a big deal of sitting really far away from us and bringing perfume that she sprayed in our direction when she got on. That perfume was probably what was making Jake sick, if you ask me. Either that, or it had just become a bad habit for him. Or maybe the sight of her really did make him gag.

Anyway, besides the bad arrivals and departures, camp was awesome! I loved, loved, loved it! And what's really weird was that I'd grown so close to my Hotcakes teammates so fast. I mean Elle, Georgia, Charlotte, Caroline and Kira. I felt almost as close to them as I do to Mia, Katie and Alexis. It's weird. I guess it's because we spent so much intense time together, and we chatted all we wanted (unlike at school, where we actually have to shut up in class and learn!). I think Alexis feels the same way.

Oh, and it was true that we had the best team. We got Raoul and Maryanne to admit it. Sydney's team was the worst because according to her counsellors, by way of *our* counsellors, every day she made a different girl on her team cry. Can you believe it?

The week seemed really long because of all the newness, so by Thursday night I was pretty wiped out, but Alexis and I had to bake for camp's Cupcake Friday. The other bummer was when Mia called to see if we wanted to go to the cinema. (Her stepfather, Eddie, was treating.)

Now, the thing about the four members of the Cupcake Club is that when one of us proposes an activity or a plan, the only thing that really prevents us from doing it is if it's something random, like a sibling's birthday or someone's grandma is visiting. Because we all know one another's schedules so well, we don't even bother proposing plans unless we know all four of us can make it.

So Mia and Katie knew Alexis and I were technically free Thursday night. Except that we weren't. Because we were baking for our new friends. Ugh.

When Mia called I was speechless. Of course I wanted to go, but I also didn't want to let down our new friends, especially when everyone had made such a big deal about our cupcakes. I mean, our team was basically named after our cupcakes! So I ended up kind of lying and telling Mia I was really tired and couldn't go, but that I could do it Friday after we baked. But Mia said we really wouldn't have time to do both. She was kind of bummed and a little annoyed when she hung up. I'd never turned down a plan before.

I wanted to dial Alexis to warn her, but I knew I'd get busted, what with Mia calling at the same time. (I could just picture Alexis: "Oh, hang on, Mia, I have Emma calling on the other line." Yikes!) So I sat by the phone and waited for it to ring, which I knew it would.

"Hi," I said, drumming my fingers on the kitchen counter. I could see from the caller ID that it was Alexis.

"Whoops," she said.

"I know. Major whoops. What did you say?"

"I said we had relays today and I was tired, but I could do it tomorrow."

"Me too! I said basically the same thing!" I love Alexis. She and I have just always been on the same page, ever since we were little.

"Phew," she said. "But I think she was mad."

My heart sank, remembering. "I know."

We were quiet. Finally I said, "Oh well, when are you coming over?"

Alexis said she'd be over soon, so I hung up to await her arrival, and began making bacon for my trademark bacon cupcakes with salted caramel ribbons. It sounds gross, but they're one of our bestsellers. I always make extra for Matt and Sam, because they love them.

I busied myself in the kitchen until, at last, Alexis came in. She took one look at me and flung herself dramatically across the kitchen table.

"What?" I asked. My heart was thumping. Had the others found out?

"They know," she whispered.

"Whaaaaat? How?"

"I confessed," she whispered again. It was almost like she didn't want me to hear her.

I sat down heavily in a chair. "Why? How? When?"

"I called Mia back and said we wanted to bring in cupcakes to camp tomorrow – I didn't say who asked us – and that maybe if they wanted to come to your house tonight, we could all bake them together." She cringed.

"So does Mia know we weren't telling the truth before?"

Alexis nodded.

I put my head in my hands. "We shouldn't have lied."

"I know." Alexis sighed. "Honesty is always the best policy. Especially when it comes to friends. But they are coming. We decided we'd bake the samples and the usual batches for Mona tonight and go to the movies tomorrow instead." She grinned at me.

"Alexis! You tricked me! So they aren't mad?"

Alexis shrugged. "A little, but I think they understand. I offered to let them take some cupcakes with them for tomorrow, too."

Katie was taking an intensive cooking class (it was actually for older teens but they made an exception for her because of her skill and passion and, I think, the Cupcake Club). Mia was working as an intern for her mum, who was a fashion stylist on photo shoots. Very glamorous. She'd go to sleepaway camp later in the summer.

"Wow, you are some negotiator," I said.

Alexis beamed and did a fake Sydney-esque hair flip.

"I'm not thrilled about delivering two-day-old cupcakes to our best client, though," I said.

"I know, but every once in a while we can make an exception," said Alexis.

"I guess. But let's pinkie promise not to do it again for a really long time, okay?"

Alexis stuck out her pinkie and hooked it with mine, and we shook our hands from side to side. "Okay."

It was a little awkward when Mia and Katie came, but I apologized and explained, telling them why I'd felt nervous to admit our plan. They

37

were mad at first and told me so, but we made up and then it was fine. One of the great things about old friends is they can forgive and forget. Little incidents become tiny in the scheme of longer friendships.

We made new samples for Mona, baked up her minis, and made the frosting, putting each into separate Tupperware containers to keep them fresh. I'd assemble them Saturday morning before I dropped them off. Mia teased me and said it was my punishment for lying.

The cinnamon bun cupcakes turned out delicious, and I knew Mona would love them. I couldn't wait for her to try them.

I was up early Saturday morning, putting the finishing touches on Mona's delivery, even though I was a little tired. The movie the night before had been awesome, and we'd run into a couple of girls from camp. It was actually fun introducing Mia and Katie to Charlotte and Georgia and watching them chat, like two different worlds mixing! Mia and Katie were really pleased when the Hotcakes girls made a big deal about the Cupcake Club and admired how the Cupcakers were such best friends and moguls-in-training. I think then that Mia and

Katie realised Alexis and I will always love them best, even if we have new friends at camp. I would always choose my old friends over my new ones. No matter what.

After Mona's cupcakes were ready, my dad gave me a ride to The Special Day on his way to drop Matt at football practice. He was going to round-trip it and then wait for me downstairs. I was looking forward to my trip to Mona's and to some time alone in that all-white plush palace of hers, even if it was for just half an hour.

I was surprised to see that all the assistants were already there. Usually, the few times I'd gone with Alexis to make the delivery (like, if I'd slept over at her house the night before), it was really quiet. The store stayed open late Friday nights to accommodate people with busy work schedules, and Mona didn't open to the public until ten on Saturday mornings.

But today, the store was buzzing, even though it was only nine o'clock. Patricia, Mona's number-one assistant and store manager, came whizzing over to greet me. It was weird. She seemed like she was kind of in a rush to get me out of there. She looked outside the door to make sure no one was behind me, then she locked the door after me. It was like she was nervous other people might be trying to come in.

I said, "Hi, Patricia! I have our delivery, and we also—"

Patricia, who was normally supersweet and patient, interrupted me. "Thanks, Emma. Okay, then, we're all set. Let me just get your money. Wait right here. . ." She took the carriers from me and headed to the back of the store. Usually we carry them back to the counter, and they pay us out of the register. I stood there in confusion.

"Do you need help?" I called lamely after her.

"Got it!" she kind of whispered back at me.

What on Earth was up?

Just then Mona stepped out of the largest and fanciest of all the salon rooms (called the Bridal Suite) and pulled the door tightly closed behind her. Was there a client in there already? Mona was really dressed up, even for her, and she looked even busier than usual. She strode over to a rack to select something, and then she spied me.

"Emma!" she cried, putting her hand to her chest, like I'd given her a fright.

"Hi," I said, smiling awkwardly.

"Is Patricia helping you?" she asked urgently.

"All under control," Patricia trilled nervously.

40

"Um, Mona, we brought some new kinds of cupcakes for you today, on the house. We were just thinking you might be tired of the usual order, okay? So just let us know . . ."

Patricia came bustling back to me with the cash. "Okay, then, we're all set. Thanks so much." She took my arm and steered me to the door.

"Patricia, is everything okay?" I suddenly got nervous that maybe they were being held up at gunpoint or something. I'd seen that on a TV show one time, where the robbers made the store employees carry on as usual, even while they were holding one of them hostage in the back of the store. "Are you being robbed or something? Should I call 911?" I asked under my breath.

Patricia stopped in her tracks and took a good look at me, then she collapsed in laughter, her hands on her knees. Mona rushed over.

"What is it, Patricia?" she asked.

Patricia was trying to catch her breath. "Oh my," she said, wiping her eyes with a tissue from one of the many boxes in the store (brides' families always cry when they see the brides in their dresses for the first time). "Just an attack of nerves," she said, still mopping. "Emma, you are too much. No, we are not being robbed. We are fine." She glanced at

41

Mona, seeming to ask a question with her eyes.

Mona stepped in and spoke in a low voice. "We have a very exciting, very private client here this morning. We opened early for her, so she could have the place to herself. It's just a little nerve-racking, but very good. Thank you for your concern, sweetheart." She turned to Patricia. "Isn't this one just divine?" she asked.

"Divine," agreed Patricia.

Just then the door to the Bridal Suite opened, and out walked the biggest surprise of my life.

"Oh my goodness!" I gasped.

CHAPTER 5

Me, Model?

Our town has only ever produced one major celebrity, as far as I know, and it made a superstar. It's like the town saved up its potential star power, and instead of launching a handful of B- or C-list one-hit wonders and soap stars, it stockpiled all its fairy dust for one lucky young lady: a gorgeous, blonde Academy Awar –, Golden Globe – *and* Emmy-winning actress named Romaine Ford.

Every girl in America wanted to be her and every guy wanted to date her. Every father wanted his son to marry her, and every mum approved. She was twenty-nine years old, wholesome, smart, beautiful, talented and reportedly very nice. She did charity work all over the world, recorded hit songs with famous costars, and was a Rhodes Scholar –

whatever that is. I'd only seen Romaine Ford once in real life, when she came to town to be the grand marshal for a parade a few years back. I knew, of course, like the rest of America, that she was now engaged to the devastatingly handsome heartthrob, actor Liam Carey, and that she planned a wedding in a top-secret location for late this summer. She was just about the last person I ever expected to see here this morning.

"Hi!" she said, friendly but a little reserved. She was wearing one of the white velour robes The Special Day gives you to put on in between dresses, and white fluffy slippers.

I was speechless. I think my jaw was actually hanging open.

"Yes, Ms Ford, what can we do for you?" said Mona, hustling over to her side.

"I just had one thing I forgot to tell you. Um, my niece, who is also my goddaughter, is going to be a junior bridesmaid for me. I'm supposed to find a dress for her, and I wonder if you could help with that, too."

"Of course, we will bring in a selection immediately. Patricia!" Mona all but snapped her fingers at Patricia, who was standing, like me, frozen, like a deer in the headlights. Patricia came alive and started across the store to where the bridesmaids' dresses were.

Romaine was still standing there, actually kind of looking at me. She was so beautiful, I couldn't help staring. Her hair was long and thick and yellow-blonde (natural, supposedly), and her eyes were wide and blue. She had a huge, almost goofy smile, and big white teeth, with a big dimple in her left cheek and freckles on her nose. She was tall and thin, in great shape, of course (she climbed Mt. Kilimanjaro last year to get ready for a part, and she did orphan relief work while she was there. Thank you, *People* magazine!), and very graceful.

Mona spoke to Patricia again. "Patricia! Emma!" She gestured at me.

Patricia smacked her forehead hard. "Right. Sorry." She doubled back to let me out of the store first. She went to unlock the door, but Romaine interrupted the silence with one word.

"Wait!" she said.

We all turned to stare at her.

"Sorry, but . . . that girl looks a lot like my niece. And I was wondering, maybe, would it be possible for her . . . I mean, do you have the time, sweetie? Would you be able to try on a dress, so I could see what it actually looks like on a girl?"

Would I? I looked at Patricia, who looked at Mona. Mona seemed to weigh the options, then found herself in favour of the idea. "Certainly. Emma, come."

"Do you have time?" asked Romaine as I started across the expanse of white carpet towards her.

I didn't trust myself to speak, so I nodded, wide-eyed, as if I was in a trance. As if I wouldn't have time for *anything* Romaine Ford asked me to do!

"Oh good!" she said, sighing. "Being a bride is a lot of work. I wouldn't want to fall down on the job and not get the junior bridesmaid's dress right!"

I couldn't imagine Romaine Ford not doing everything perfectly. I also had a hard time picturing any girl not being so happy to be in her wedding that she just wore whatever Romaine told her to. Like a trained puppy, I followed Patricia to the rack, where she selected a few dresses and wordlessly held them up against me to see if they'd fit. Finding four, she led me to a dressing room and gestured that I should go in.

"Call out when you have one on, and I'll come pin it if need be."

I looked at myself in the mirror in the dressing room. Was I dreaming? Had I imagined all this? Was I really going to model dresses for

Romaine Ford because she thought I looked like her niece?

I pinched myself – actually pinched myself – to make sure I wasn't dreaming, then I put on the first dress, quickly but carefully. I know from being a bridesmaid before that these dresses are very fragile and very expensive, but I knew I had to be fast, for Mona's and Patricia's sakes.

"Ready!" I called. Patricia flew into the room and started pinning wildly.

"There!" she declared, taking a long appraising look at me in the mirror. "Let's put up your hair. It will look much neater." Then finally she said, "Okay. Ready."

Patricia led me out into the salon and then knocked on the door of the Bridal Suite.

"Come in!" Mona trilled, and we entered.

Huge fluffy wedding dresses hung from every available rod and pole, and others were draped over the white sofas and chairs. Mona's fanciest silver tea service was laid out on the white lacquer coffee table. There were four women gathered around the table, sipping from fancy china teacups.

"Oh my! You really *do* look like Riley!" said an older blonde woman who must've been Romaine's mother.

"I told you!" said Romaine proudly. I smiled shyly.

"Ladies, this is Emma Taylor, our cupcake baker and former client. She has a few dresses to show you, so let's see what you think. This first one is a hand-crocheted lace from Belgium. It truly is one-of-a-kind and, as such, one of our most expensive junior bridesmaids' dresses at eighteen hundred dollars."

Eighteen hundred dollars! I nearly fainted! My bridesmaid dress for Mia's mum's wedding had cost $250, and I thought that was a lot! But Romaine and her group seemed unfazed by the crazy price. I remembered Romaine had earned ten million dollars for her last movie, a big drama where she played a famous queen from the sixteen hundreds. Talk about earning power! *Alexis, eat your heart out,* I thought.

"Very pretty," said Romaine's mother.

Another lady (her grandmother? Her agent?), who was older than the woman who spoke earlier, said, "Yes, and you look lovely in it, dear."

Romaine was looking at me with her head tilted to the side, considering. "Yes, you look fab, and the dress is so pretty. I wonder . . . Would you think I was rude if I asked to see you with your hair down, like it was before? I'm sorry. I just think with the hair up, it's more of a mature look . . ."

I nodded and looked to Patricia for help. She took right over. "Absolutely. Of course. So right. A natural look is always much better for this age," she said, and she hurriedly undid her previous work and fluffed out my loose hair with her fingers.

"Ahh! So pretty!" said a girl Romaine's age. I think it could have been her sister. According to *Us Weekly* magazine, she has three sisters and a brother.

As the minutes wore on, I thought I'd explode if I had to wait any longer to tell my friends about this. I kept my composure, though, turning this way and that as they admired the dress. A few minutes later they were ready to see the next dress, and I returned to my fitting room to change.

Patricia undid the back of the dress for me and tactfully left the room. I wouldn't be able to do this if I had to change in front of everyone, but as long as I could do it privately, it was okay. I called Patricia back in to help with the buttons, and we did the modeling all over again.

Between dresses number two and three, I rushed to the phone to call my dad to tell him I'd be late. I didn't tell him why. It wasn't that I thought he'd call the paparazzi or anything, but I wanted the experience to be complete before I started blabbing. Maybe it wouldn't end well, or maybe it would. Who knew? It was still just a private event, though.

My dad was fine with a later pickup, and in the meantime, Patricia stood behind the counter and organised the cupcakes on a beautiful silver serving tray to take in to the ladies.

"Remember," I said, "some are different. We included cinnamon bun cupcakes with cream-cheese frosting. Mona hasn't approved them yet."

"Oh, I noticed that some of these looked different than usual," said Patricia. "Well, let's give them a whirl. Maybe they'll be a huge box-office hit!" She popped one into her mouth, and chewed. "Oh, Emma! These are just . . ."

"Divine?" I offered.

We laughed, and she delivered the cupcakes while I changed dresses again.

In dress number three, I took a hard look at myself. This was not such a pretty dress. Even I could see that it was too grown-up for me. The dress was made from a slinky material, with a low-cut front and a slit up the leg. I wasn't comfortable in it at all.

Patricia returned. "Hmm," she said. "It's not right for you. But you know how people dress in Hollywood. I think we should show it, anyway."

She pinned it into place and then led me back into the room.

"NO!" said Romaine as soon as I walked in.

I was taken aback, and it must've shown on my face because she hurried to apologise.

"Oh my gosh, I'm so sorry, sweetie! I scared you!" She jumped up and came over to pat my arm sympathetically. "I just have really strong reactions to young girls dressed inappropriately. I just hate it. I was reacting to the dress, not to you. You poor thing! I forgot for a moment that you're not a professional model! Are you okay? Did I scare you to death?"

I composed myself and laughed a little, but she *had* shaken me. It must be hard for models and actresses to remember that their audiences aren't reacting to them personally, but rather to the outfits or the performances. It would take me a while to get used to that.

In the meantime, Patricia passed around the platter of cupcakes. Romaine scooped one up (from my kitchen to Romaine Ford's mouth! The Cupcakers – not to mention my brothers – would die, just die, when I told them!) and popped it into her mouth.

"Oh my gosh! What are in these cinnamon ones? I love them! They're so insanely delicious!"

Mona looked very pleased. "Emma made them, as I said earlier. She and her friends started their own business baking cupcakes."

"You do?" said Romaine. "That's so entrepreneurial! I was like that at your age." Alexis would love to hear that!

Back in the fitting room, I changed into dress number four. It wasn't much of a hit either. It was kind of *Little House on the Prairie* style, with long sleeves and a smocked front. Kind of country. Romaine didn't like it.

Mona was all business. "We have a trunk show scheduled for next Saturday, with all sorts of new dresses and accessories coming in this week for it. They are absolutely gorgeous and all brand-new, never-before-seen designs. We could arrange for you to come in at the same time and have a private showing, if you're available?"

Romaine's group all consulted their Black-Berrys and iPhones, and agreed. Mona turned to me. "Emma? We'd love for you to return, if you're free?"

I nodded happily. "Sure. No problem. I can come. I'll bring the cupcakes, too."

"Yum! Thanks!" said Romaine. She came and gave me a hug good-bye, careful not to squash the dress. "See you next week," she said. "Thanks for all of your help! You were a doll!"

On my way out, Mona asked me not to mention next weekend's plan to anyone. She said it was fine to say what happened today, but they wouldn't want any gawkers hanging around next weekend if word got out. I felt really privileged to be in on the plan, so I promised I wouldn't tell.

I couldn't believe the morning I'd had.

CHAPTER 6

Now *I'm* a Celebrity!

(O)kay, so start again from the beginning, when you first saw her open the door. How did you know it was her?" Katie asked.

Mia, Katie and Alexis could not get enough of the story.

"No, tell about when she said she was entrepreneurial like us when she was a kid!" begged Alexis.

I had told the story three times already today, and I knew I'd tell it again to a very receptive audience at camp on Monday. I almost wanted to stop now, to keep it fresh for the Hotcakes girls. I just laughed.

"It was amazing," I said, shaking my head. It was like a dream.

"I can't believe you didn't get her autograph!" said Mia morosely.

"I can't believe Mona didn't pay you!" said Alexis.

"Oh my gosh, I probably would have paid her!" I laughed.

"You are so lucky," Katie said with a sigh.

"Do you think you'll ever see her again?" Alexis asked.

"I hope so," I said. I was dying inside since I couldn't tell them about the plan for next weekend.

"If they call you back, maybe we could all go?" asked Katie.

I laughed again. "Let's cross that bridge if we come to it."

"*When* we come to it," said Alexis. "Confidence sells!"

Monday morning at camp was almost more fun than Saturday morning at The Special Day. All the Hotcakes were riveted as I told the story of Romaine Ford. Even Maryanne and Raoul. Raoul kept asking if she was as pretty in person. And Kira was so excited, it was crazy.

"Oh my gosh, she has been my idol ever since I can remember. You are so lucky, Emma. You know, she lived on my block when she was in primary school. I've always felt like she was my soul sister or something. She's been my role model and my inspiration! She's just an amazing and generous person, and the fact that she is from here, that she went to the same schools as me! I just worship her."

No one noticed Sydney Whitman until it was too late. "What are you Hotcakes yapping about?" Sydney managed to sneer whenever she said the word "Hotcakes."

"Just that Emma modelled for Romaine Ford this weekend," Alexis said.

Sydney's head whipped around. "No way! You? Modelling? That can't be true!"

I nodded, never happier in my life than while seeing this bomb being dropped on Sydney, despite her disbelief that I could ever model.

"Wait, *the* Romaine Ford?" Sydney was still incredulous.

"Uh-huh!"

"Oh, wow! I can't believe it! I'm going to *be* her in the talent show! I'm singing 'Sweet Summer Love,' that duet she had with the country singer, old what's-his-name, you know! I'm singing that!"

"Wow," I said. "Small world." Leave it to Sydney to make it all about her.

"Everyone says I look a lot like her, you know.

Everyone says I'll grow up to be just like her."
Sydney posed while we all stared at her like she was
an alien.

"Really," said Alexis finally, more like a state-
ment than a question.

"Yes!" said Sydney. "Really!"

"Well, good luck with that!" I said cheerfully.
I wasn't going to let Sydney "Horrible" Whitman
ruin my day by taking over my story and making
it about her.

Maryanne came over to tell us it was time for
softball, so we ditched Sydney to follow her to the
field.

"Listen, what is everyone doing for the talent
show?" asked Maryanne as we walked.

"I'm using a Hula-Hoop!" said Elle. She was
such a cutup. We all laughed. "No, really! I'm serious. I'm great at it! It's my little-known talent!"

"That will be great!" said Raoul enthusiastically.
"I can help you with music and choreography if
you like." He was a big dancer. The two of them
started scheming and laughing.

Charlotte and Georgia were going to do a gymnastics routine, and Caroline was going to sing. She
was in her church choir and, according to Elle, was
so good that she regularly sang solos. A few other

girls, like Tricia and Louise, told us their plans, and then Maryanne looked at me and Alexis.

"How about you two?" she asked. "What about a bake-off?" Our cupcakes had been a huge hit on Friday. I think she was just angling for more to sample.

"We'll definitely bring some cupcakes, but as for the show, I'm not a talent myself. But I am happy to be a talent manager," said Alexis affirmatively.

"I don't have a talent. Anyway, I'd die of embarrassment up there," I said.

"How about the flute?" Alexis suggested. She turned to Maryanne and the others. "Emma's really great at the flute. She plays in the school orchestra. You should do that, Emma."

"I'm not that good. And, anyway, I don't play alone. It's one thing to be part of a big group when you're onstage, but *alone*? No way."

Alexis turned to Maryanne. "I can see I've found my first client. Don't worry. I'll get her to do something."

It was not going to happen, but I didn't want to embarrass Alexis by not letting her at least pretend she could convince me.

"Just remember," said Maryanne, "there are three qualities they're looking for in the talent show: *Talent*, like how good you are at the thing you're doing. *Presentation*, like, are you confident, is your act polished, and did you think through your moves and your programme? And finally, *charm*. This is how appealling the crowd finds you. Do you have that certain charisma audiences love? Each performer is rated in each of the categories on a scale of one to ten. Whoever has the most points wins overall, but there's also a winner in each of the three categories."

Alexis leaned back and whispered, "We're going overall, baby. Shoot for the moon."

She was already talking like a Hollywood agent. I laughed and hit her playfully. "Get real!" I said.

"Oh, I'm real, my friend. I am really real."

The bus ride home was one of the more annoying rides of my life. For starters, Alexis would not back off from the idea that I was going to play the flute in the talent show, and she decided that on this bus ride, she would convince me she was right. In the course of one mile, she moved from asking to demanding I do it, and she was only half joking.

To make matters worse, Sydney asked if I'd brought any baby wipes to sanitise things after Jake threw up. Jake yelled, "I'm not a baby!" and then started to cry, so that was fun. *Not*.

Alexis decided to cheer up Jake by asking him what kind of cupcakes he wanted for his birthday. But he couldn't make up his mind. First he said, "Vanilla, with vanilla icing. That's what my friends and I like."

But, annoyingly, Alexis couldn't leave it at that. She said, "Oh, come on, Jakey, make it a little harder for us. Don't you want a fun topping? Or a cool design? What's your favourite, favourite thing on Earth to eat?"

So Jake moved from one flavour to the next: chocolate, banana, s'mores, cinnamon bun and caramel. They discussed Oreo topping, marshmallow frosting, SpongeBob colours, police badge designs and on and on. By the end of the ride, Jake was more confused than when we started. As she stood up to leave the bus, Alexis promised, "Jake, these will be the yummiest, best-looking, coolest Jake Cakes anyone has ever seen. I personally guarantee it," and I wanted to scream at her for setting his expectations so high.

And then, walking backwards down the aisle, she called out, "An announcement, everybody: Emma Taylor is playing the flute in the talent show. Emma, practise your piece tonight! Bye!" Then she ran off before I could actually kill her.

All the kids on the bus turned to look at me, and I had to kind of smile and nod and acknowledge what she said. I wanted to die with all those eyes on me.

There was no way I'd play in that talent show!

CHAPTER 7

Shoved into the Spotlight

*T*he weekend couldn't come soon enough! All week I felt butterflies in my stomach every time I pictured going back to The Special Day, but I couldn't tell if they were happy butterflies or nervous butterflies. It was like I dreaded and looked forward to it the same amount. On Friday night at our cupcake meeting/baking session, I couldn't stop thinking that we were baking for Romaine Ford!

We finished the cinnamon bun minis for Mona, and the extra vanilla/vanilla minis. Then it was time to bake samples for Jake.

"I had a great idea for Jake's cupcakes, so I went ahead and brought the supplies," said Mia, pulling a plastic grocery bag out of her tote. "Are you ready?

Dirt with worms!" She held up a package of Oreo cookies and a bag of gummy worm candies.

I groaned. "Gross!"

"He'll love it!" said Katie, clapping.

We had some extra batter from Mona's minis, so we baked up a few full-size cupcakes, and Mia set about crushing the cookies.

Alexis said slyly, "We have a talent show at the end of our camp session, and Emma is going to play her flute!"

I rolled my eyes. "I am not."

"Oh, Emma! You should! You're so good!" said Katie.

"Why wouldn't you?" asked Mia.

I started ticking off reasons on my fingers. "Well, for one thing, I'm not that good. For another, I have nothing to wear. Third, I hate getting up in front of people, and I also hate having people look at me. And fifth, I don't have any 'charm,' which is another thing they score you on, so all in all, I'm not doing it."

My three friends stared at me. Then Mia said, "Wow! You've got it all figured out, I guess. But why are you so down on yourself?"

"I'm not down on myself. I just know what I'm good at and what I'm not good at."

"Well, couldn't you practise a piece? Isn't there anything you know well enough?" Katie asked.

"That's not the point!" I said. I crossed my arms to show I was annoyed. I felt like they were ganging up on me.

"The other reasons are just silly," said Mia. "You could wear the bridesmaid dress from my mum's wedding. That looked amazing on you, and then it wouldn't be just hanging in your closet until you outgrow it."

Annoyingly, she was right. I wished she hadn't solved that problem so easily.

"And you obviously don't hate getting up in front of people that much, since you did it for Romaine Ford last week, for goodness sake!"

"That's different," I said, blushing.

"Why? Wouldn't you think a professional performer is a tougher critic than a bunch of parents who think you're adorable and little brothers who are just waiting for the show to be over so they can eat some cupcakes?" said Mia, laughing now.

I hadn't thought of that either. "But what about charm? I don't have any charm!" I insisted.

Alexis interrupted. "That is something I can take care of for you. That shouldn't worry you one bit. Anyway, it's not like you'd be trying to win *all three* categories. No one does."

I thought you said we were to "shoot for the moon," I wanted to remind Alexis, even though I didn't want to encourage her. Instead, I huffed and looked away from my friends. They were making it really hard to keep refusing. And now that they'd sort of solved all my qualms, a tiny part of me was starting to problem solve the rest, and think about how I could do it. But . . .

"How can I compete against Sydney Whitman? I know she's going to win, anyway, so why bother?"

Mia pressed her lips into a thin line of disapproval. "That is just a bad attitude right there. You're way more charming than she is, for one thing. Anyway, what is she doing?"

"Singing that Romaine Ford country song," I mumbled.

Katie burst out laughing. "Have you ever heard Sydney *sing*? Wake up, people! I am here to tell you that she was in my music class last year, and the girl cannot sing a note! It was like listening to a dying hyena!" Katie started howling tunelessly, and we all began to roar with laughter.

We finished our samples for Jake, packed up Mona's minis, and cleaned up. By then it was time for the others to go home.

Mia gave me a hug good-bye and said, "You've got to do the talent show, Emma. Even if it's just to beat out Syd the Hyena. Do it for us. Do it for the Cupcake Club!"

"And don't forget to let us know what Jake thinks of the dirty cupcakes!" added Katie.

I laughed and shut the door.

Upstairs, I looked for something to distract me from the butterflies that had returned, and I spied my flute, lying in its case on my desk. I sighed, then crossed the room, picked it up and set it up to play. I have to admit that as I played, a whole hour passed before I even realised it. I really do love playing the flute. Just not in front of a crowd.

The next morning, I was up at the crack of dawn to shower and blow-dry my hair. Mona had e-mailed to confirm the timing (I had to be there at eight thirty, cupcakes and all), and she reminded me to appear "natural," meaning no makeup, no fancy hairstyles or anything. It was hard to resist the temptation to tinker, but I managed.

Down in the kitchen, I discovered Jake eating worm cupcakes for breakfast. He loved them so much, he tried to hug me, but I dodged him – chocolate crumbs and all.

My mum dropped me off, leaving my dad in charge of the boys. She asked me if I wanted her to wait outside and read a magazine, but I knew I couldn't let Mona down by spilling the beans (not that my mum would call the paparazzi, but still). I told her I had some work to do with Mona, to choose the flavours for the next month, and that she should come back later.

When I reached the store, the door was locked, so I rang the bell. I could see all the attendants bustling around inside. Patricia was putting big vases of white roses on every available surface. The two other ladies were dusting tables and fluffing sofa cushions. Mona heard the bell and made a beeline for me at the door.

"Darling! You look divine! It's so good to see you and your tiny cupcakes! Come in, come in!" She shooed me inside and locked the store's door tightly behind me, just as Patricia had done last week.

I brought the cupcakes to the counter, and she paid me and then led me to an even larger changing room than before.

"Now, a few things before we begin," she said. "First of all, I have this for you." She handed me a full-length nude-coloured slip.

"Put this on to wear for the whole time. It will give you a clean line under the dresses and make the fabric move right, and it will protect your modesty. This way Patricia can be in the room arranging the next dress as you take one off."

That was a good idea. I wondered how she knew I hated to change in front of other people?

"Everyone hates to change in front of other people, darling," said Mona, reading my mind.

"Next, some tips. Stand up straight, straight, straight. No slouching. Let's see . . . Hmm . . ." She pulled my shoulders back and tipped my chin up into a kind of awkward pose. "I know it feels strange at first, but it looks wonderful. See? Divine!"

I looked in the mirror and saw that she was right. The pose made my neck look longer and kind of elegant.

"Now don't forget to smile, darling. Smile so your eyes sparkle. Let's see it."

I smiled, but she didn't approve.

"No, that's more like a grimace. Think of a princess or a movie star, how their eyes kind of light up. Lift your eyebrows a little. Be happy! Try again. Yes. Better." She turned my face to look in the mirror. Then she did different smiles next to me while I practised.

68

"Good. Better. Yes, much better. Now, most important of all, don't forget to breathe. Just take deep breaths and think your happiest thoughts. Think about cupcakes and your divine friends and all the fun you'll have this summer. All right?"

I nodded and mentally reviewed her list of directions: stand up straight, shoulders back, chin up, smile with sparkly eyes, breathe and think happy thoughts. Okay!

I heard the doorbell ring, and Patricia trilled, "They're here!"

Mona and I looked at each other with excitement. "Good luck, darling. You'll be smashing!" And off she ran.

Smashing. Divine. Oh my gosh! Here we go!

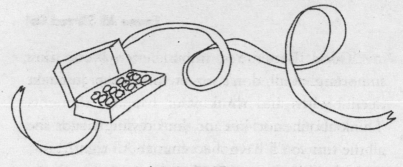

CHAPTER 8

Hard Work and a Good Deed

𝒟id I mention that modelling is really hard work? You have to do all those things Mona said, plus you're wearing a dress that might be itchy or heavy or too big or too small or loaded with pins that could stab you anytime. You have to get used to people saying they think what you're wearing is ugly or too expensive, that you should take it off immediately. Also you can get hot and hungry and even bored, no matter if your audience is a major star who is beautiful, nice and interesting.

But I still had a blast!

Romaine was even nicer this time, if that is possible to believe. First of all, she remembered my name. She said, "Hi, Emma!" when I walked in, and jumped up to give me a double kiss, like they do in Europe. Then she ate a bunch of my cupcakes and complimented me on them, even pretending to faint when she took a bite.

Patricia helped me in the dressing room the whole time, and we got to chat about everything. I told her all about the talent show and how the Cupcakers want me to do it and that they told me to wear my bridesmaid dress. She thought I should totally go for it, and was surprised when I said I didn't have the guts.

"But you're so poised doing this! Why wouldn't you just treat it the same way? It's like work. You just go out, you do your little routine, you turn around and you leave the stage. That's it! It's great practise for real life, because when you're an adult, you do end up having to get up in front of people and perform, for all different occasions and reasons."

I thought about it while I twirled around the Bridal Suite in a tulle-skirted dress that made me look like a ballerina. Romaine tried to get me to do ballet poses, and we started joking around. It was really fun. She'd make a good teacher.

Mona hustled me back to change, though, whispering we were running out of time to keep the store closed to the public. I loved all the dresses I had tried on, so the time had flown. I was sad when I put on the final dress, and I think Patricia could tell.

"It was fun, right, honey? Kind of like being a princess for a day? That's how brides feel when they come in too." She gave me a little pat on the back and sent me into the Bridal Suite for the final time.

Romaine walked over to me to inspect the dress. Meanwhile, in the background, her mum and her aunt were talking. My ears perked up at the word "cupcake."

"Kathy, are you thinking what I'm thinking about these cupcakes?" asked Romaine's aunt.

"Yes, I think I am. They are *so* delicious!" said Romaine's mum.

Turning to me, Romaine's aunt said, "Could we hire your cupcake club to bake some cupcakes for our bridal shower? I'm Romaine's aunt, Maureen Shipley, and I'm the hostess for the event. These would be lovely for the dessert."

Oh my gosh! Could this day get any better? Somehow I found my voice.

"Absolutely. Showers are our specialty! I'll give you my card when I go back to the fitting room," I promised. I silently thanked Alexis for insisting we each have our own business cards made.

In the fitting room, I carefully changed back into my now pathetic-looking everyday clothes. I grabbed a business card from my bag and went to say good-bye.

Romaine saw me in the doorway and jumped up. "Oh, Emma, honey, you were the best! Thank you so much for your hard work today and last week. It was such a treat to have you here, and you are just gorgeous. Adorable. Right, Mum?"

Romaine's aunt said, "Honey, let's get a photo, so we can all remember the fun we've had together." She pulled out her camera and had Patricia snap a few shots, including one of just me and Romaine together. Then she double-checked she had my e-mail address and promised to send me the photos.

I was sad to leave – I don't think any of us wanted it to be over – but I knew Mona was eager to open the store, so I said my good-byes and headed out of the Bridal Suite. Before I reached the front of the store, Mona caught up with me. She slipped a white business envelope into my hand.

"Emma, a little something for all your hard work."

"Oh no, Mona, I couldn't. Thank you. It was so much fun and such an incredible experience."

"I insist! From one businesswoman to another.

Please take it. Fun or not, it was hard work, and you were divine! Just divine!"

It's hard to argue against a force of nature like Mona, so I laughed and thanked her for the opportunity to model.

Outside, who should I run into walking by but Kira and her oldest sister!

"Hi, Kira!" I said, still flying high after my fun morning.

"Hi, Emma! Oh, Leslie, this is my friend Emma who I was telling you about, who got to meet Romaine Ford! Emma, this is my sister Leslie. She's taking me to get a new swimming costume. What are you doing here?"

I felt funny telling them what I'd been doing. But as it turned out, I didn't need to. Because who should come strolling out of The Special Day but Romaine and her group.

"Oh, look who's still here! Bye, honey!" said Romaine's mum.

I waved, smiling.

"Bye, Emma! Thanks again!" called Romaine with a smile.

"Oh my gosh!" said Kira, her jaw dropping open. "That's her! And she knows your name! Oh my gosh! I think I'm hyperventilating! Oh my gosh!"

She started fanning herself, and tears welled up in her eyes. "I can't believe it's really her."

Romaine and her mum, aunt and sister were all standing outside The Special Day, as if deciding where they should head to next. Impulsively, I grabbed Kira's arm and quickly dragged her over to Romaine's side.

"Romaine, I'm sorry to interrupt," I said. "But this is my friend Kira. She thinks you are so great, and I wanted you to meet her." I kind of shoved Kira towards Romaine. Kira was in shock, her mouth still wide open and speechless.

Romaine was very friendly. "Hi, Kira! It's nice to meet you! Any friend of Emma's is a friend of mine! Are you in the same class at school?" she asked politely.

Kira couldn't talk. She just shook her head no and continued to stare, wide-eyed at Romaine.

Romaine looked at me and giggled, then looked back to Kira. "How do you two know each other?" she asked.

"Oh, camp. We go to day camp together," I said, since it was clear that Kira wouldn't be able to answer. "Right, Kira?" I prompted.

Kira closed her mouth, and gulped. "Uh-huh. Camp."

"What camp is it?" asked Romaine.

"Spring Lake Day Camp," I said. Kira nodded.

"Oh my gosh! I went there in sixth grade!" cried Romaine. "Mum! Emma and her friend go to Spring Lake Day Camp!"

Romaine's mum smiled. "Oh, what fun! You loved that place!" she said.

"I really did. Well, have a great time there. I have to get going now, but it was nice to meet you, Kira, and thanks again, Emma!" She gave me another hug and then walked away. Kira was still rooted to the spot, speechless.

Leslie came up and showed us a photo she'd snapped on her iPhone of Kira and Romaine chatting.

"Oh wow!" said Kira, coming back to life, as if she'd been in a trance. "I can't believe it! I just met Romaine Ford! Oh, Emma!" She wheeled around to face me. "You're the best. I feel like I dreamed the whole thing."

Leslie was laughing at her now. "Come on, dreamy. Let's go find you a swimming costume. Bye, Emma!"

"Okay, bye! Nice to meet you, Leslie!'

They called their good-byes and strolled off, Kira staring intently at Leslie's iPhone.

I was so glad I'd done what I did. It wasn't the smoothest thing in the world, but it had obviously meant a lot to Kira, who in general needed a boost. I was just happy to have provided it.

I texted my mum for a ride and sat down to wait. What a great summer this was turning out to be!

CHAPTER 9

Hotcakes and Cupcakes

Camp was out-of-control fun. For starters, because it was separated into boys' and girls' campuses, there wasn't a lot of worrying what boys would think or even, for me, dealing with boys' gross-out behaviours like I did at home. It was a complete break from burping and stinky socks and football. I was in all-girl heaven!

We sang all the time, whatever we were doing. Show tunes, Top 40 songs, camp songs – anything. We braided one another's hair during free time, and one day Georgia brought in a manicure set and gave us all wild, decorative manicures, with tiny flower and star decals and stuff. We also made friendship bracelets like maniacs, taping the embroidery thread to any available surface and twisting, braiding and tying it into rainbows to wear or give away. We had Tie-Dye Day, when we brought in anything from home that we wanted to tie-dye and made incredible designs with bright colours, like a kaleidoscope. (I brought white drawstring pj bottoms, plus, the camp gave us each a white cotton T-shirt.)

We had also started to seriously train for the Camp Olympics. There would be events in archery, swimming, diving, track and field, canoeing, not to mention football and softball games, hand ball, tetherball and relay races (some of them funny, like potato-sack and egg-on-a-spoon races). Not everyone had to participate in every event; you just needed enough people from your team to do it. So Maryanne and Raoul were working on how to divide up everyone and play to their strengths.

Every morning we'd gather at our rally zone and chat about what had happened in the fifteen or so hours since we'd last been together (covering TV shows, celebrity gossip, family news – anything, really). Kira was always there first, her wet hair pulled back into a neat ponytail. Leslie dropped her off way early on her way to work. Alexis was a pretty early arrival too, and Georgia and Charlotte, so they'd all be up to speed by the time I arrived with the the rest of the bus crew.

I was not wild about canoeing or softball, so I didn't plan to participate in those events, but Maryanne and Raoul felt they would have a pretty good team for softball even without me. I volunteered to be the water girl for that game. I was psyched for the running events, because I am fast, and I was feeling really good about the swimming and diving, which I knew I'd ace (not that I'd ever say it out loud). The only bummer was that the swim events required six-person teams, so we could only really field one team from the Hotcakes, with Kira being a noncompeter in that category. We were all really careful not to make her feel responsible, because we didn't want her to feel bad. Alexis and Elle both said early on that they didn't want to do the swim competition (I think they planned it for Kira's sake, because they are both great swimmers), and a few other people said they didn't care either way, so I was on the team that would compete.

The Hotcakes were pretty good athletes, if I do say so myself. Plus, we were training hard. We did warm-ups, calisthenics, drills and had little mini-competitions within our team. We cheered on everyone's progress all the time. It felt great to be part of a group like this, where everyone was fun and they had your back. Kind of like the Cupcake Club, but all new.

Meanwhile, Sydney was being a nightmare. She was so determined that the Angels would win the whole competition that she was tormenting her teammates to train harder and harder. It would have been funny if she wasn't so awful. Sometimes we Hotcakes just stopped and stared while she lit into one of her teammates. It would only last a moment, until one of her counsellors rushed over to put an end to it, but it was still just unbelievable.

One day, after track-and-field training, we were all hot and sweaty, and we jumped in the pool with our clothes on. Maryanne and Raoul were kind of annoyed at us at first, but then they saw how much fun we were having and they jumped in with their clothes on too! It was hilarious. Afterwards, we hauled ourselves out and stretched out on the grass, drying off in the sun and talking about our summer plans.

That was when Elle announced that her birthday was coming up, and her plan was to have a party with all the Hotcakes, at her house! It sounded like a blast. She would have us over, we'd eat pizza, and the night she planned to do it, there was an outdoor movie showing in a park downtown, so we'd all go with blankets and watch the outdoor movie and eat treats. Then we'd go back to her house and sleep over. Everyone said they wanted to go. But when she told me the date, my heart sank. It was for a Friday night – the night before the Camp Finale Talent Show, actually – and that was, of course, the Cupcake Club's special baking night for Mona.

Alexis and I looked at each other, knowing what the other person was thinking. It was not going to be easy to tell Mia and Katie that we couldn't make it on a Friday night because we were doing something without them. And we'd pinkie promised not to sell Mona two-day-old cupcakes again.

We tried to discuss it later on the bus home, but Jake was in one of his moods.

"Stop talking, Emmy! I'm trying to sleep!" He moaned, his head against my upper arm.

Alexis and I tried to whisper. "What do we say? Do we tell them the truth?" I asked.

Alexis shot me a look. "Lying didn't do us any good the last time."

I sighed.

"Stop breathing hard, Emmy! It's making my head bounce!" wailed Jake.

Alexis shot me a sympathetic look. I tried to remain calm, but all I wanted to do was chuck him out the window.

That night, while I was practising my flute piece (I hadn't decided yet whether I'd perform, but I was at least taking care of the talent part by getting a piece in order), my mum tapped on my door. As the only girl in a mostly boy house, I have a strict knocking policy and a big KEEP OUT sign on my door.

"Come in!" I called.

"Oh, honey, I love to hear you play. You're so talented," said my mum. She always says that when she comes in while I'm playing. "Just play a little bit more for me."

She settled into my armchair, which is big and cushy and covered in the prettiest white fabric with sprigs of pink flowers on it. She put her head back, closed her eyes, and smiled.

I played the piece through from beginning to end, and she said, "Again," without lifting her head or opening her eyes. I shook my head and laughed, but I played it again.

My mum's eyes opened and she sat up. "You play the flute beautifully," she said. "I'm so proud of you."

"It's pretty fun," I said, shrugging. "I'm thinking about playing that piece in the camp talent show."

"Oh, you have to!" said my mum. "It would be lovely!"

"I don't know, though. I'd hate to have all those people watch me. And ... well ..." I didn't have the dress excuse anymore, or the talent excuse, because the piece was sounding pretty good. But how do you tell your own mother that you have no charm and expect her to leave it at that?

She tilted her head to the side. "So?"

"Well, I might play. That's all."

"I suggest you go for it. What do you have to lose? Everyone will be impressed. Is it a competition or just a showcase?"

"Well, there are prizes, so I guess it's a competition."

"What kinds of prizes? Like first, second, third place?"

I shook my head. "No, like categories: talent, presentation, charm and all-around winner."

My mum put her hand up for a high five. "You could definitely win!"

I high-fived her weakly. "Which category?"

"Any of them! All of them! If I was the judge, you'd take home all the prizes."

We laughed. "Thanks," I said.

"It seems like you're really enjoying camp," said my mum.

"Yeah." I smiled. "I love it. And I've made so many good, new friends. . . ." I bit my lip.

"Wait, why do you suddenly look so sad?" my mum asked with a laugh. "It's like someone just flipped a switch! I thought you were happy!"

"I am. It's just . . ." I proceeded to fill her in on the conflict for Elle's party and the Cupcakers, as well as the incident a couple of weeks ago when Alexis and I had to bake for our camp friends.

"Cupcakes, Hotcakes . . . How do you keep all these people straight?" My mum was smiling. "Seriously, though, I agree with Alexis. Look, the sleepover is a onetime thing. These are new friends; they might not be lifelong friends. Or they might be, who knows? You just need to let Katie and Mia know that they come first, but on this one special occasion, you want to go to this special event. And just make a plan to do something fun with them on a different night. I think it will be fine. Old friends are very important, but you have to have room in your life for new friends, too, right?"

I sighed. "Yeah. I just wish they could all be friends together," I said.

My mum thought for a minute. "Then maybe you should figure out how to make that happen!"

Hmm. Maybe she had a point! I thought about it for a second.

"Wait, maybe I should have them all over – like not *all* the Hotcakes, but maybe just Elle and Kira? Along with the Cupcakers? That could be fun!"

My mum smiled and lifted her hands in the air, palms up. "Why not?" she said enthusiastically.

I reached across and gave her a hug. "Thanks, Mum. Great thinking."

"Oooh! Those words are music to my ears!"

CHAPTER 10

Friendship, Favours and Flute Practice

A week had passed before I got the e-mail from Mrs Shipley, Romaine's aunt, but it was a doozy, in good ways and in bad! The good parts were, it had three great photos from The Special Day attached – one group shot and two of me and Romaine that were amazing! (I instantly made it my desktop background!) And it had an order for ten dozen mini cupcakes!

The bad part was that the shower was going to be on a Saturday morning – the morning after Elle's Friday night party *and* the same day as our camp's talent show. Now, it's one thing to bake a day in advance for Mona, a regular customer. But I did not want Romaine Ford's cupcakes to be anything less than fresh and perfect. For starters, it was

Cupcake Diaries

such a big job, and it might lead to other big jobs. Our cupcakes had to be at their very best that day!

I forwarded the e-mail to Alexis and then called her.

"Hi, Emma," she answered. She also has caller ID, so she knew it was me.

"Hey. Did you see my e-mail?"

"Just opening it. Wow, great photos! Oh, the order! Goody! Oh. Not goody. Hmm."

"I know."

We sat there in silence, thinking.

"Well, we could get up early and bake Saturday morning?" she suggested.

"I guess," I said. "It's cutting it a little close. I mean, ten dozen cupcakes! We'd have to leave Elle's at, like, six in the morning."

"Hmm," said Alexis.

"It's too bad we couldn't have Mia and Katie bake the cupcakes Friday night, then we get together at, like, eight o'clock Saturday morning and do the frosting and delivery."

"That would be kind of mean. Like, 'Hey, we're taking the night off, but why don't you two do this big job for us, and we'll catch up with you later?'" said Alexis in an annoyed voice.

I had to giggle. "But maybe we could ask them.

Maybe we'll just offer them something in return – a night off, or whatever. And we *are* helping Katie for her cooking class's bake-off, remember?"

Alexis sighed. "I guess."

"Honesty is the best policy, remember?"

"I'll call a meeting," said Alexis.

The next afternoon, we had an emergency Cupcake meeting at Mia's house. Alexis hadn't told Mia and Katie exactly why we needed to meet (she just said we had major scheduling issues), so they were a little in the dark.

Alexis wasted no time in calling the meeting to order. "First topic on today's list, Jake's birthday party. Emma, please confirm the details."

"Well . . . Jake loved the dirt with worms cup-cakes! He said they were his 'most favouritest ever.'"

I rolled my eyes while Mia and Katie said, "Awww . . ."

I continued, "His party is next Saturday after-noon, so we can bake Friday night and then assemble Saturday morning. They have fourteen boys coming – my worst nightmare – so they'll need four dozen cupcakes, accounting for Matt and Sam and various babysitters and parents."

Alexis interrupted me. "Now, if you'd like, Emma and I can handle the baking on Friday and give you girls the night off. We'll do Mona and Jake all in one marathon session, and you two can, like, go out or something." She tried to look really casual as she said this, but I could see she was nervous.

Mia and Katie were confused. "Where would we go without you guys?" asked Katie, her eyebrows knit together, like she didn't understand.

"Yeah, why wouldn't we want to do the baking for the Jakester?" asked Mia.

"Well, I was just saying. I mean, maybe we don't all need to be there . . ." said Alexis, shrugging.

Honesty is the best policy, I reminded myself. I took a deep breath and plunged in. "Guys. The weekend after that, Alexis and I were invited to a sleepover on Friday night by our friend Elle from camp. Our whole team is going. But, drumroll, please, Romaine Ford's wedding shower is the next day, and they ordered ten dozen cupcakes!"

Mia and Katie squealed and jumped in the air. They hugged each other, then me, then Alexis, who received them awkwardly. She was still nervous.

"Oh, Emma, that is so awesome! I can't wait to meet Romaine Ford!" said Mia.

"I know." I smiled.

"It's just a bummer that you have to miss your sleepover," said Katie.

Gulp.

"Um . . . well . . ." I looked helplessly at Alexis. She wouldn't meet my eye. "We were actually thinking, maybe . . ."

"Oh! Wait! I get it!" said Mia, who is usually much quicker on the uptake. "You'll give us the Friday before off, so we'll work while you're at the slumber party."

I nodded, feeling like an idiot.

"Wow," said Katie. "Um . . ."

"The other thing is, I'm having a sleepover at my house the night before Jake's party. It's for the Cupcake Club and two of my friends from camp, Elle and Kira. It's going to be really fun, and I won't do it unless you two will come," I said impulsively.

Alexis's head whipped to the side and she stared at me with a question in her eyes.

There was a pause in the room that seemed to drag on forever. Then Mia said, "You know what? We'll do it. Right, Katie? That's what friends are for."

I looked at Katie. She still had kind of a hurt, skeptical look on her face. I knew this would be hardest on her, because of the Callie/Sydney history.

"Katie, we're not going to dump you for our

camp friends. I promise," I said quietly. "They're fun, you'll see, but they're not like the Cupcake Club. It's not at the same level, and it never will be." I knew in my heart that that was true. Once school started again and the Cupcake Club was together every day, I knew I'd drift a little apart from Elle and Kira.

Katie took a deep breath in and then sighed. "Okay. I understand. New friends are great, really. I'm just so cautious ever since Callie."

Mia hugged her. "We know. Don't worry. You'll always have us hanging around, right, Cupcakers?"

"Right!" Alexis and I yelled, then we piled in for a group hug.

It was settled. Now I just had to break the news to my mum about the sleepover.

Okay, that last part didn't go so well.

"Wait, the night before Jake's party you want to have a sleepover for six friends? Are you joking?" said my mother in exasperation.

"Well, actually, it's five friends, plus me. So that's not so—"

She interrupted me. "I'm sorry. I don't care how many friends it's for. There is not going to be a sleepover the night before we're having fifteen

92

six-year-olds running all over this house for the day. You'll have the whole house up all night, you'll have the place a mess, and Jake will be overtired for his party, not to mention me!"

I was starting to fume. The worst part was, I could kind of see what she meant.

"You're the one who had the brilliant idea to get all my friends together from camp and school!"

"Not for a sleepover on that particular night I didn't!" she said firmly.

I knew I wouldn't win this one, but I couldn't face undoing the plan. I'd be so embarrassed. After all, Kira and Elle barely knew me when it came right down to it. They might think I was nuts or that my mum was a mean psycho.

"How am I going to tell everyone they're uninvited, then?" I said. I knew I was being bratty, but I didn't care.

"Just like that. You're uninvited!" said my mum with a toss of her head. "Think of a new plan," she said, and she stormed into her bathroom to take a shower.

I left her room and went into mine, slamming the door behind me. When my anger had cleared, I sat and thought about all the things that were coming up and needed attention.

There was the Camp Olympics, which our team was pretty well set for. There was another superjocky team of girls, the Wolverines, who would probably give us a run for our money, but it wouldn't kill me to lose to them, in that they were so athletic and talented. I just wanted to make sure we beat Sydney's team.

Next, there was Jake's party to bake for and survive. It was going to be hard work.

Then there was Elle's slumber party, my non–slumber party and Romaine's shower – they were all tied up into one big snarl that needed untangling.

And finally, there was the Camp Finale. Was I in or not? And if I was in, where was I going to find some charm? Time was running out.

CHAPTER 11

Cupcakes, Meet the Hotcakes

$\mathcal{R}$aoul passed around an official sign-up sheet the next morning at camp.

"Okay, girls! Everyone needs to sign up and give a description of their act. They're printing the programmes this week, so this is final. If you're in, you're in, and if you're out, you're out, but don't make the mistake of being out!" He laughed. "We've got a lot of talent in this group, and I know my Hotcakes are going to bring home the gold!" He pumped his fist in the air, and everyone cheered.

When the clipboard reached me, I stared down at it, unsure and paralyzed. Suddenly, Alexis reached across, grabbed the clipboard and quickly wrote down my name. Then she wrote "Flute

Performance" and passed the pen and clipboard to the next person. She folded her arms across her chest and smiled at me smugly.

I just shook my head slowly from side to side. Finally I said, "But what about charm?"

"Leave it to me," said Alexis, but she didn't look too confident.

I had already e-mailed Alexis, Mia and Katie the bad news about Friday's sleepover. We'd just have a regular baking session instead, so that was okay. But all morning I had been dreading uninviting Elle and Kira. I had a pit in my stomach and could think of nothing else. Finally, at lunch, Kira said, "I can't wait for Friday night! Should I bring an air mattress?" Alexis and I looked at each other, and sighed.

"Guys, I have bad news. My mum said no sleepover on Friday," I admitted, wincing at the mum reference. (I had been avoiding any mention of mine when I was around Kira.)

"Oh, don't worry about it!" said Elle with a wave of her hand. "No problem." She took a bite out of her sandwich, unfazed. Elle was a trooper, and I loved her for it. She didn't even need an explanation. "You're still coming to mine though, right?" she asked, through a mouthful of turkey.

"Yes," I said. "The problem with my sleepover plan is, it's my little brother's birthday party at our house the next day, and, well, my mum said we'd all be exhausted if I had a sleepover the night before. I could do it another time, though."

"Bummer," said Kira. I could see that she'd been looking forward to it.

"I know." I wondered if she understood, not having a mum and all that.

"But maybe we could still do something?" Alexis suggested brightly. "Like maybe the girls want to come bake Jake's cupcakes with us!" she said with a smile.

"I'm not sure how much fun that would be, with all that work?" I said, glaring at her. What was she thinking? It would be boring for Elle and Kira, and what would Katie and Mia think about us inviting non-Cupcakers to join us at work? But before I could say anything, in jumped Kira and Elle.

"We'd love to!" said Kira enthusiastically. "That would be so fun!"

"I'm in," said Elle with a grin.

"Ookaaay . . . Great, then!" I said, faking confidence. "You guys can just come home on the bus with me from camp." I'd let Alexis do the explaining to Mia and Katie since it was her idea.

❀

Just as I suspected, Katie was not thrilled. I guess she felt threatened by our new friends and kind of resentful of them and the time they got to spend with us all day while she was with a bunch of strangers at her cooking class. I totally understood, but at the same time it couldn't always just be the four of us, could it?

When Friday rolled around and we all showed up in my kitchen, things were a little awkward to say the least, even though everyone had been prepared in advance for the new plan.

Mia was nice, if not all that chatty at first. But Katie was downright cold. I saw Elle and Kira exchange a look of confusion after Katie basically said hi and turned her back on them, but Alexis, bless her heart, kept on chattering away to make up for it. I had brought Jake home from camp and settled him in front of the TV, and my other two brothers would be home soon to look after him.

We set out the ingredients and told the new girls what we were doing. Alexis designated Kira as the Oreo smasher and Elle as the cupcake-liner person, meaning she'd set the papers into the baking tins. Alexis had found awesome camouflage patterned cupcake liners in green, so that's what we were using for the Jake Cakes, as we were calling them.

Katie busied herself at the mixer, and Mia and I were working on the frosting. Alexis was setting out the necessities for Mona's minis, which also needed to be made. It was a regular assembly line!

Elle started telling funny stories about camp, and that kind of broke the ice. Mia offered up some stories from the fashion world and Kira was really interested in that. But the more they chatted, the more withdrawn Katie became. I knew she was insecure, but it was really annoying me, and rude. Finally, I stood up to talk to her in private, but right then my older brothers came crashing through the door in their usual noisy style.

"Hey, Cupcakers! What's up!" called Sam. Did I mention that Sam is gorgeous? All my friends basically pass out whenever he is around, which makes me feel kind of proud and kind of annoyed. He's a lot older than us (seventeen) and not around that much, but he's tall with blond, wavy hair and bright blue eyes like my dad. Plus, he's superathletic, so he's in really good shape. He also likes to joke around.

"Ooh! Cake Mix!" he said, spying Katie at the mixer.

"Not so fast, mister!" said Katie, covering the mixer with her arms.

Elle and Kira were just watching, speechless. Neither of them had brothers, of course, so these guys were like aliens to them.

Meanwhile, Matt, who, I guess, is also pretty good-looking (according to Alexis, with her on-again off-again crush on him), was talking to Alexis and Mia, teasing them about camp and cupcakes and everything, trying to get them to give him gummy worms and promise him the first cupcakes out of the oven.

It was kind of total boy chaos, but Sam and Matt were making my old friends laugh and making a big deal out of them. I interrupted to introduce Elle and Kira, and although my brothers were polite, they went right back to teasing the Cupcakers.

Finally, I shooed them out, and they went in to take over the TV from Jake. The room was very, very quiet after they left. Katie was standing at the mixer, smiling to herself, Kira and Elle were wide-eyed and Alexis and Mia were still laughing.

"Phew!" I said. "Those two are a nightmare!" I was kind of embarrassed by all the commotion.

"No, they're not!" whispered Elle, her eyebrows raised up high on her forehead. "They're gorgeous!"

"And they're in love with all the Cupcake girls!" Kira sighed, genuinely wistful. "You're so lucky!"

"Aw, no, they're not," protested Mia and Alexis, but they were pleased.

Katie looked up, unsure if Kira was for real, but when she saw that Kira was serious, she allowed herself to smile at her. My anger at Katie melted a little bit then.

"Seriously," said Elle.

Then Jake came running into the room, crying about how the big boys had taken over the TV and changed *SpongeBob* to *SportsCentre*. He ran straight to Mia, buried his head in her legs and wailed.

Mia scooped him up and began to soothe him, but he whined that he wanted Katie, too, and wouldn't settle down until the two of them were fawning over him, feeding him gummy worms and setting him up with a little workstation of his own.

I was apologetic and mortified, but Elle and Kira were just bowled over by my brothers and how much the boys loved my Cupcake friends.

"You girls are so lucky," Kira said admiringly. "Especially you, Emma, to have all these boys around all the time."

"Ha! As if!" I laughed.

But I could see Katie smiling out of the corner of my eyes.

Against all odds, my annoying brothers had broken the ice. Hotcakes and Cupcakers united as the afternoon wore on, and by the time my parents got home at six and ordered pizza for everyone, we were well ahead of schedule on both baking jobs. All us girls were sitting around the kitchen table, laughing and talking, as the boys periodically wandered in and out and caused silences and then outbursts of giggles. It was so fun!

At the end of the night, Kira pulled out her phone to call her sister for a ride. I could see Katie looking at her with curiosity. Just as I realised what Katie was thinking, it was too late.

"Why does your sister pick you up instead of your parents?" she asked.

I winced and looked down at my hands. I didn't know what to say.

Kira bit her lip. "Well, my mum died last year, and my dad travels for work all the time. I mean, he has to. That's his job. So, I have three older sisters, and they take turns taking care of me."

"Oh, I'm so sorry. I didn't know," said Katie. And to her credit, she was visibly upset.

"That's okay," said Kira graciously. "Thanks."

"I'd love to have three older sisters!" I said, to change the subject.

Kira groaned. "No, you wouldn't! They are so bossy!"

"It's true!" agreed Alexis. "Older sisters are the worst!"

And just like that, things were back to normal. We chatted as we put the finishing touches on the cupcakes. Too soon, Kira's sister was at the door, and we all hugged good-bye, with Mia and Katie even hugging Elle and Kira!

After they left, it was just the Cupcakers in the kitchen, waiting for Mia's stepdad to come pick them up.

"Wow, those girls are really nice!" said Mia. "I'm proud of you two for going out in the world and finding such nice new friends for us all," she joked.

Katie agreed. "Yeah, and I'm sorry I wasn't very friendly at first. I was just shy, and I felt like, you know, you were kind of replacing us with those two."

"It's okay," I said, putting my arm around her shoulders. "And don't worry. You're irreplaceable!"

That night my mum came to tuck me in.

"Good job, lovebug," she said. "It was really nice

to see all those girls getting along and having such fun. You're a great judge of character, and I love your friends. I'm sorry about the sleepover, but I'm glad you worked something out."

I snuggled under my pink duvet. "I know, Mama," I said, using my baby name for her. "It was really nice. Thanks for the pizza!" I yawned.

"See? Wasn't I right? Aren't you glad you're not lying on the TV room floor in a sleeping bag for the next three hours, giggling?" She gave me a kiss on the forehead.

"Yes. I actually am," I said.

And I was.

CHAPTER 12

Happy Birthday, Jake!

Take fifteen six-year-old boys, add fifteen water guns, two hundred water balloons, mud, tears and lots of junk food, and what do you get? Total chaos. That was Jake's party.

I had invited Mia, Alexis and Katie to help with the party. My mum was actually paying us to help wrangle the kids, keep the refreshments going and stay on top of the garbage and cleanup. We also had to guard the doors, so the kids didn't end up inside watching TV or trashing Jake's room or anything.

For me, the best part was that Mia, Alexis and Katie got to sample what my life is really all about. There was no time to be squeamish when one kid gashed his foot open. There was nowhere to run when Jake's friend Ben picked up a toad and brought it right up to us to see. Replenishing the snacks and drinks was an endless task. The minute a bowl of Cheetos had been filled, the bowl of chips was empty and needed to be refilled, and so on.

As the party wore on (only two hours had passed!), Mia, Katie and Alexis began to look more and more bedraggled and overwhelmed. When Jake and another kid got into a fight over whose water gun was whose, my friends were horrified.

"But they're friends!" said Katie, observing the chaos with a hand to her mouth. "Why do they fight like that? Look, that guy is punching Jake!"

"I know," I said. "That's what boys do. They just work it out on the spot and move on. Hey! Guys! No hitting! Use words!" I called, to no real effect. I shrugged.

"Wow, Emma. I had no idea," said Mia.

"Yeah, how cute do you think Jake is now?" I asked.

We all looked at him. He was covered in mud, his hair was soaked and sticking up all over, and he had a scratch on his arm from a tree branch (it was bleeding). He had orange Cheetos dust all over his face and had on ratty clothes. Well, they were ratty now. They didn't start out that way. And he and his buddy Justin were saying horrible things to each other as they yanked a water gun back and forth.

Suddenly, Jake realised we were looking at him. He let go of the water gun, leaving Justin to collapse in a heap, and came over with a big, sweet smile on his face. "Where are my cupcakes, girls?" he asked.

"Awww ..." said Mia and Katie, melting all over again.

I rolled my eyes and then looked at my watch. "Five more minutes," I said. "Go back and play, and be a good host! Let your guest have the water gun he wants!" I watched to make sure he did, then I turned to the girls. "Shall we?" I asked.

We went inside to get the cupcakes, candles and camera, as well as the party plates and napkins. Outside, the boys saw us coming and swarmed us. "Down, boys! We'll call you in just one minute. We're not ready yet!"

"Oh wow!" said Mia, laughing with shock as she held the cupcake platter high above the boys' heads. "They really are savages!"

"See?" I said. "Okay, guys. We have to light the candles and then sing." The boys were busy forming themselves into a straggly line, insisting who was first and second to get cupcakes. I started a rousing rendition of the birthday song, and everyone joined in. Jake looked cute as everyone sang, then he blew out his candle and the crowd surged.

Suddenly, Jake yelled, "STOP!" at the top of his lungs, and miraculously, everyone stopped. Jake smiled, then said, "Let's give a cheer for my big sister, Emma, who is the best! She and her friends all made these cupcakes for us and they are going to be awesome! Yay, Cupcake girls!"

All the little boys cheered and applauded, and there was nothing for us girls to do but take a bow. I turned to smile at Alexis, and I saw she had a funny look on her face, the one she gets when she has an idea. I couldn't begin to imagine what she'd be thinking of now, but I was just glad to see she, Mia and Katie were happy and Jake was having a ball. All in all, a great party!

It took forever to get the backyard and kitchen back in order. But the Cupcakers were great. They'd stayed late to help clean up, then flopped on the couch to watch TV afterwards. We were pooped. They said it gave them new respect for me, living with all those boys.

"See?" I'd said. "I told you so!"

The week after Jake's party, no one at camp could talk about anything but the Camp Olympics and the talent show. We trained for our sporting events like we were in boot camp, and at home I practised my piece and took out my bridesmaid dress for my mum to press. I was nervous about the charm portion, but Alexis was assuring me she had it all figured out. That kind of scared me, but since I didn't have any better ideas, I had to just let it go.

Sydney was like a slave driver to her team, totally dissatisfied with their performances as the time of the talent show drew near. We watched in horror as she yelled at one girl after another for what she considered their bad performances, and we discussed in whispers the rumour we'd heard that Sydney would not be permitted back at camp for the second session.

Finally, it was Friday!

The Hotcakes got to camp early and warmed up, stretching and dancing to great music. We were pumped. Raoul and Maryanne had brought us cereal bars and yogurts to keep up our energy.

The games got off to a great start, with an awesome, three-inning softball game, which we won! Tricia hit an amazing home run, and Louise knocked a double that brought in two runners. I kept the water coming, and before we knew it, the game was over and we were at the track for relays and sprints. This was my moment.

I lined up alongside the other girls my age in the first heat of the first race: a five-hundred-yard sprint. Elle was running too, and so was Charlotte. To my left was Sydney. Nothing could make me run faster than that.

The camp director blew the whistle, and we were off! I didn't look to the left or the right. I just pumped my arms hard and lifted my legs high, and I ran like Sydney Whitman was chasing me. Which she was. After I crossed the finish line (first! Yay!), I looked back, and Sydney was still about twenty yards back. I had beaten her handily and so had one of her teammates, a girl she'd repeatedly yelled at for being slow.

"Nice race, girls!" said the camp director as three of us were given medals for first, second and third place. Sydney crossed the finish line and then pouted, tossing her hair. I heard her saying to someone that there had been a "false start," and she hadn't been ready, so that race didn't really count. I had to just shake my head.

Our team did well through the track-and-field events, and we had a lead heading into the swimming. We trooped over to the pool as the boys' teams exited, and I saw Sydney trying to chat up a bunch of boys who were clearly having a hard time figuring out what to do or say. Their heads were in the game, but they were interested in her. They just didn't know whether to stay and talk or keep on walking. I almost felt sorry for them.

At the pool, the Hotcakes huddled for a pep talk and a strategy meeting, and Raoul, with a huge smile on his face, asked for our attention.

"Chicas, I have some very exciting news. We will be fielding two swim squads today, after all." He grinned.

Everyone looked around in confusion and chattered while he called for silence.

"One of your teammates has made an extra effort so that everyone would be able to participate in these events. Kira has been coming to camp early all month to work with Mr Collins, and she is ready to bust out her new moves in the pool today and show you all what she can do!"

I looked at Kira in shock. She was smiling shyly as everyone congratulated her. I thought back to her early morning drop-offs and the wet hair, and was annoyed at myself for not figuring it out sooner.

"Oh, Kira! I am so proud of you!" I cried, and I threw my arms around her in a hug.

We assembled for the relay: two squads, with three swimmers from each at either end of the pool. I noticed Kira was swimming from the deep end, which would be easier for her. If she started to fail, she'd be in the shallow end. But I needn't have worried.

When Mr Collins blew his whistle, the swimmers dove in and took turns swimming the length of the pool. Kira was in the final heat of the relay, and because her team was a little rusty, she wound up swimming alone, dead last. But she dove into the pool and glided, and the Hotcakes were silent until she surfaced. Then we went wild, screaming and cheering until we were hoarse. We walked the length of the pool with Kira as she swam, encouraging her all the way. Her stroke wasn't perfect and she wasn't that fast and her team obviously did not win, but it was, for us Hotcakes, the sweetest victory we could ever have imagined. We mobbed her when she got out of the pool, and Maryanne was there with a towel. Kira was crying, and it was the best, best moment of my whole camp experience. It was right then that we all felt we'd won the Camp Olympics, no matter what.

I saw Sydney on the sidelines, looking perplexed, and I was glad she had no idea what was going on. We'd kept this issue private, and we'd celebrate Kira's triumph among ourselves, just the Hotcakes. That was the way it should be. I couldn't have been happier if our team had won every race. Friends were more important than medals, and I was so proud of my new friend Kira. I'd always heard the expression "It's not whether you win or lose; it's how you play the game." But now I finally understood it – and it's true.

CHAPTER 13

Hotcakes to the Rescue!

Well, we didn't win the Camp Olympics overall. The Wolverines did, but that was to be expected. The Angels came in dead last. They were so far behind the rest of us that I had to wonder if Sydney's team mutinied against her and decided to lose on purpose. I would have if I were on the Angels. Still, the Hotcakes came in second, and that was good enough for us. The celebration of Kira's victory continued into Elle's sleepover, and we all toasted her with ginger ale at the movie and again back at Elle's house, when we had a snack before bedtime.

Elle's party was a blast, and for me and Alexis, it cemented our friendships with the summer gang. Even though most of us didn't live in the same part of town – some of us didn't even live in the same town – we knew we'd get together throughout the rest of the year and stay friends forever.

On Saturday morning, Alexis and I were up and packed by seven a.m. Her mum had promised to bring us to Katie's so we could finish frosting the cupcakes. My mum would pick us up from there, after dropping Matt off at football, and take the Cupcakers first to Mona's, then to Romaine's aunt's house. *Then* we'd head home to change for the big talent show! I couldn't even think about that last part – I was so nervous. Plus, we had so much to get through before it came time for that.

While we waited for Mrs Becker, I checked my e-mail on Elle's family computer in her kitchen.

"Oh no!" I said. I couldn't believe the e-mail I'd just received.

"What?" said Alexis, hearing the alarm in my voice.

"Mrs Shipley e-mailed yesterday, but obviously I didn't get it in time. She wanted to know if we could put daisies on the cupcakes 'cause it's a daisy-themed shower!" I looked at Alexis with horror. "How will we ever have time?"

"Time for what?" Kira yawned, straggling into the room. She was dressed but looked sleepy.

Alexis and I looked at each other in a panic, trying to think. "We need help," she said finally.

"I'll help you!" offered Kira.

"I'll help you with whatever it is too," said Georgia, who'd just come into the kitchen.

Pretty soon we had all of the Hotcakes offering to help us.

"Assembly line?" said Alexis with a smile.

"Totally," I agreed.

With a quick call to Katie and to Mrs Becker, we rearranged the plan so that Mrs Becker would pick up Katie, Mia and all the supplies, and bring them to Elle's, where ten helpers awaited their tasks.

It wasn't an hour before everyone had a spot in Elle's kitchen and dining room, and we were frosting cupcakes and piping flowers onto them, chatting and working hard. Everyone was ecstatic to be working on cupcakes Romaine Ford might eat, so they were taking extra care that things looked perfect.

Mia and Katie were very gracious about the whole change of plan, and Elle even apologised to them, saying, "I'm so sorry I didn't think to invite you two to sleep over, since you're honourary Hotcakes. Next time, you two are at the top of my guest list!" I was so happy to see my friends becoming friends.

Finally, everything was ready and packed to go. My mum was outside in the minivan waiting for us, and the Cupcake Club said our good-byes and thank-yous to everyone. Kira was looking at us so wistfully, and all I could think of was how excited she'd been to meet Romaine at the mall. I whispered a quick question to the Cupcakers, and everyone nodded enthusiastically in reply. So I said, "Hey, Kira, want to come, and we'll drop you off afterwards?"

It only took her a nanosecond to process what I meant, but then she cried, "Do I?" and ran to get her things. After all of Kira's hard work for the team, she deserved a special treat like this.

After running Mona's cupcakes to her, we immediately took off for the far side of town and reached Mrs Shipley's right on time. There was a catering van parked in her driveway, and a few other cars — one of them looked really fancy, like the kind a movie star might drive — so I hoped that meant that Romaine was there.

Nervously, the five of us carried the cupcake bins to the back door. I rang the bell, and Mrs Shipley herself came to the door.

"Oh, Emma, hello! And this must be the Cupcake Club! Come in, come in!"

I held my breath, waiting for someone to point out that it was the Cupcake Club plus one, but to everyone's credit, they didn't say anything.

"Here we are! Daisy cupcakes!" I said.

"Fabulous! I'm so sorry that was such a last-minute idea, but ooh goody! Let's see!"

We lifted the lid from the cupcake carrier and showed her our work. The cupcakes did look adorable.

"Oooh! Wow! Kathy! Come see!" she called.

Mrs Ford appeared in the kitchen doorway, decorating supplies in hand. "Hi, girls! I'm Kathy! Hi, Emma, honey, how are you?"

I knew my friends were impressed that these ladies all knew me, and I did feel a little proud, I have to say. But the main thing we were all wondering was, would we get to see Romaine?

And then, "Mum?" I heard her voice!

"In here, honey! Emma's here!"

Mia and Katie nudged me with excitement, their eyes sparkling. I had to smile.

"Emma! And cupcakes! Yay!" Romaine was in the doorway and came over to give me a big hug. I was grinning from ear to ear, and I knew I was blushing. I felt kind of like a dork, but I was proud.

"Hi, girls! Is this the rest of the Cupcake Club?" asked Romaine, superfriendly. "Hi. I've met you before! At the mall, right?" she said to Kira. Kira just about died of happiness.

She nodded.

"That's Kira," I said, taking charge of the introductions. "And this is Mia, Katie and Alexis."

Everyone said shy hellos, and Alexis congratulated Romaine on her wedding, remembering to mention Liam Carey's name, which I thought was a nice touch.

Then Romaine looked at the cupcakes, and squealed, "I love them! Oh my gosh! They are so pretty!" Then she looked at me with a sneaky expression. "Can I try one?" she asked.

"Go ahead! They're all yours!" I said.

"Mmm! Oh, delicious!" said Romaine through a mouthful of crumbs.

"Speaking of which . . ." Mrs Shipley handed me a white envelope that said CUPCAKE CLUB on it. "Here's your payment."

I was almost inclined to refuse it, for the honour of baking for Romaine, but Alexis reached out and took the envelope. "Thank you," she said graciously.

"She's our CFO," I said, laughing.

"Good for her! She's doing her job!" said Mrs Shipley with a smile.

Mrs Ford suggested a group photo with Romaine, and we all posed with ginormous grins on our faces, Romaine holding up a cupcake like she was about to take a bite.

"Well, we've got to be leaving now," I said.

"Can't you stay a little while longer? Could we get you something to drink?" asked Mrs Shipley, so gracious.

"Actually, it's our Camp Finale tonight. Our talent show . . . so, we need to get going . . ."

"Oh, the Camp Finale! I remember that! I did a tap dance for mine!" said Romaine. "Mum, do you remember? That was one of the best nights of my life!"

Mrs Ford winced and then laughed. "How could I forget?" She put her head in her hands. "Oh, the practising! I thought I'd never recover!"

We laughed.

"That is so fun. So who's doing what?" Romaine asked.

Alexis and I told Romaine the details, and she asked us what time it was, and what I'd wear and play, and what Kira was singing. Alexis let on that she had a special surprise planned, and while I groaned in dread, Romaine told us how excited she was for us.

Finally, we really did have to go. My mum was waiting in the car, and we knew Mrs Shipley needed to get back to organising her party.

With a long good-bye and lots of hugs, we left and tumbled back into the minivan.

We could not stop chattering. "That was so amazing!" and "She's so nice!" and "I can't believe she remembered me!" and on and on. My mum laughed, asking questions as she drove around dropping everyone off. Finally, it was just me and Alexis, who would help me get dressed for the event.

"So what's your surprise?" I asked. "You can tell me now."

"Not yet," said Alexis with a mischievous grin. "Not yet."

CHAPTER 14

Talent and Charm

The butterflies in my stomach had turned into birds by the time we got back to camp. There were so many people milling around – siblings, parents, even grandparents. I could not believe how big a crowd it was.

I had my dress in a garment bag, and I checked in backstage. The camp director handed me a programme and told me when I'd go on. Raoul was in charge of props and costumes, and he whisked my flute and dress away for safekeeping while we joined the growing audience.

"Wow. This is major," I said to Alexis, looking around. Because she wasn't performing, her parents hadn't come. She was sitting with me and my parents and brothers. But I noticed she kept looking around, like she was waiting for someone else.

Finally I said, "Who are you looking for?"

"Oh, just – There they are!" she cried, and I turned to see Mia and Katie heading right towards us. Mia had a garment bag too, and I wondered why until she handed it to Alexis.

"Here's Jake's costume," Mia said. "Hi, Jakey! Hi, Mr and Mrs Taylor." She settled in next to Alexis and started joking around with Matt and Sam. Katie smiled.

"You guys are going to be great!" she said.

"Guys?" I looked at Alexis. "Now you have to tell me."

Alexis sighed and looked at Mia and Katie in annoyance. They were so busy flirting it up with my older brothers that they missed the look. "I guess since *some* people don't know how to keep a secret," Alexis began loudly, "I will tell you our plan."

I looked at her expectantly. "This better be good, or I'm not going up there," I said.

"Oh, you're going! You and Jake, who will introduce you and carry out your chair for you to sit in. He's the charm."

"Wait, you're having that . . . unpredictable little

slob be the charm in my act?" I said. I couldn't believe this was happening.

"Yes," said Alexis definitely. "And he will not be unpredictable because he has been bribed with a whole dozen Jake Cakes, just for him. And he will not be a slob because"—she unzipped Mia's garment bag—"he will be wearing this!" She pulled out a mini tuxedo and a collapsible top hat.

I began to laugh. "Oh my gosh," I said. "Where did you get that?"

Alexis shrugged and glanced at Mia. "It helps to have connections in the fashion world."

Then everyone started to shush the crowd, and the first act began. It was a bunch of boys who were break dancing, and they were actually pretty good. I had a hard time enjoying it, though, because I was so worried about my own act to come.

Next up was a group of Wolverines who did a rap song about camp that was really funny. Some of it was unintentionally funny because they kept forgetting the words, but in the end they got a lot of applause. Elle and Tricia danced around using Hula-Hoops and were awesome, but it wasn't that much of an act. Just them twirling stuff to music. Caroline sang beautifully, and Charlotte and Georgia did their gymnastics routine, which was pretty impressive.

And then it was Sydney's turn.

The music started up, and she strode out in a cowgirl getup that was waaay too sophisticated for her. She had on piles of makeup – if I could see it from the twentieth row, you had to know it was a lot – and she kind of shimmied in time to the music as she came out. Romaine Ford would have died.

I had to give Sydney a little credit for being brave enough to come out by herself and sing. But then I thought she probably just couldn't find anyone else she thought was good enough to join her.

Until she opened her mouth. Then I realised that probably no one joined her because no one thought she was good enough.

Sydney Whitman can't sing.

At first, it was awkward. People felt bad for her, you could tell. They tipped their heads to the side, as if they were really trying to give her a good listen. But then she started doing these really hammy country dance moves, and people started to giggle. Sydney must've been pleased, seeing all the smiles in the audience. With her ego, she surely thought people were just in awe of how good she was. She began to work the audience, encouraging people to clap along with the song, which they did. And then she sang louder – she was getting progressively worse – and danced more enthusiastically, and people just started to laugh their heads off.

The funny thing was, Sydney was so blindly into herself that she never noticed. When her song ended, she gave a triumphant bow and punched the air with her first, like, "I really nailed that one!" and she skipped off stage.

Alexis, Katie, Mia and I looked at one another in shock.

"She really doesn't get it, does she?" said Alexis, shaking her head in disbelief.

Katie was smug. "I told you she couldn't sing!"

We didn't have long to marvel over what we'd just witnessed because Alexis was suddenly hustling me backstage. Mia grabbed Jake by the hand (she and Katie were going to be in charge of him), and Alexis led me to my changing area.

"Deep breaths. You are very, very talented," said Alexis as she turned her back to allow me to change privately.

"Ready," I said, even though inside I wasn't. Alexis came to zip me up and help with my hair.

I mentally went through Mona's checklist for modelling, which made me feel more in control. "Chin up, shoulders back, smile, sparkle and just breathe ..."

Mia appeared with Jake all dressed, and I had to admit, he looked absolutely adorable. Alexis hustled me to the curtain and gave last-minute directions as we stood there.

"Jake, you'll carry out the chair, put it down in the centre of the stage like you practised with your mum at home. Then you'll bow and say 'Now presenting, my sister, Emma, who will play ...'" She looked at Jake.

He nodded and said, "Beethoven's 'Ode to Joy.'"

"Right. Then you turn and hold out your hand, and Emma comes out. Then, Emma, do a little bow and sit and play. When you're done, stand up, bow and Jake will come back out to collect the chair, okay? Got it?"

"Got it!" we said.

And then suddenly they were calling my name, and it was all a blur. I remember the crowd clapping for Jake and saying "Awww ..." when he came out.

I remember sitting to play my piece and that I was amazed that that many people could be so quiet. I caught Sam's eye out in the audience at one point, and he was smiling proudly and nodding, but I had to look away.

Then it was over, and Jake was back out, and this time the crowd roared its approval as we left the stage. I was shaking so hard and smiling and so, so relieved. And most of all, I was so glad Alexis had made me do it! I felt great, like how Kira must've felt when she swam.

Backstage, Alexis grabbed me in a huge hug (so unlike her!), and so did Mia and Katie, and then I was quickly out of my dress and Jake was out of his tux. We were back in the crowd to watch the end of the show with my family. Now I could really relax and enjoy it.

I got to see Kira sing, and she had an amazing voice. I spied what must've been her dad and her sisters in the audience. At the end, her dad gave her a standing ovation and was mopping his eyes with a handkerchief. I was glad he was there for her, and he seemed really proud of her.

And finally, there was a pause at the end while the judge tallied up their results. The crowd chatted quietly among themselves as we waited.

"Cupcakers, thanks for coming," I said to the girls. "And thanks for a great summer so far."

"Don't thank us, thank the Hotcakes!" said Katie really nicely.

"It's been really fun," agreed Mia.

We talked about some of our plans for the rest of the summer and then the camp director was back onstage with the microphone.

"Ladies and gentlemen, we had a wonderful programme tonight. All these kids are so talented and worked so hard. All the participants will receive a small silver camp whistle to honour their participation. Now, the winners for tonight are in each of three categories: charm, talent and presentation. Then we do have one overall winner who nailed all three. But before we announce the winners' names, I would like to introduce a special Spring Lake Day Camp alumna who will be our presenter tonight. Ladies and gentlemen, it gives me great pleasure to introduce to you . . . Romaine Ford!"

There was a shocked silence and then the crowd erupted as Romaine came out, smiling and waving. She was in a pretty white sundress with daisies on it, and the Cupcakers and I exchanged knowing looks. It was the dress she must've worn to the shower. I craned my neck to catch Kira's eye across the crowd, and we smiled at each other and made gestures of surprise.

"Hello, folks, thank you for the warm greeting," began Romaine. "I loved my time here at Spring Lake Day Camp so when my friend Emma Taylor and her Cupcake Club told me that tonight was the Camp Finale, I just couldn't miss it!"

My friends and I all cheered and grabbed one another in excitement that she'd mentioned us. I couldn't believe it! I saw Sydney look around the crowd until she spotted us and scowled in disgust.

"Now there were some really wonderful acts I saw when I got here, and I am impressed by all of your hard work, so congratulations to all of you who performed, and to all the backstage crew who helped the performers. And here we go . . ." She looked down at a sheet of paper and began reading out the awards.

I was ecstatic when Kira won for talent. She had a lovely voice, and she was thrilled to receive the award from Romaine, who gave her a big hug and a kiss on each cheek. The magic show boys won for presentation – they'd been really organised, with lots of props and stuff – and then Sydney won for charm! I was in shock.

Romaine shook her hand graciously, and maybe I was imagining it, but she didn't seem that friendly toward Sydney. Sydney couldn't tell, though, because she was in heaven. I guess a part of me had to admit that her act *had* had a certain weird, funny charm. And at least this way she did win something, even if she was banned from attending the camp next year.

And finally Romaine said, "The all-around winner is . . . my good friend Emma Taylor!"

I couldn't believe it! It was like I was dreaming. I was up on my feet and on the stage, with Romaine hugging me so hard and rocking me back and forth. I just couldn't believe it! She handed me a big trophy and smiled for a photo Raoul took of us. She called "Good night and good luck!" to the crowd, and we walked offstage together.

Romaine was mobbed afterwards, but she managed to sneak over to my family before she left. I introduced her to my parents and my brothers, and she said hi to all the Cupcakers, remembering everyone's name!

"You should be really proud of your sister, boys," she said to Matt, Sam and Jake. "She's a very talented young woman – in the kitchen, on the runway, and onstage! Watch out, world!"

I never wanted this night to end, but it all went so fast in the end. We dropped off all the Cupcakers and headed home, just the six of us, where we sat and ate some of the dozen Jake Cakes (baked today and dropped off by Mia and Katie) at the kitchen table. (Even though the Cupcakers told Jake all twelve cupcakes were for him, he said we could share them with him.)

"Great job, honey," said my dad. "As usual."

"Yeah, honey, great job introducing us to the hot celeb!" said Sam through a mouthful of cupcake.

I rolled my eyes as the crumbs spilled out of his mouth and onto the table.

"We're proud of you, lovebug," said my mum.

"So am I!" said Jake, with a big Oreo-covered smile.

"Thanks, guys," I said. "You're the best."

I looked at my family and then thought about the Cupcakers and the Hotcakes, and meeting Romaine and all the wonderful things that happened over the summer. I had worried about fitting everyone and everything into my plans, but like a great cupcake recipe, the more things I added to the mix, the more delicious and fun everything became.

Sam, Matt and Jake were gobbling up all the cupcakes.

"Boys!" Mum cried. "We can make more! Slow down."

And then I realised that sometimes cupcakes are like friends . . . you can always make more!

Want another sweet cupcake?

Here's a sneak peek
of the eighth book in the

CUPCAKE DIARIES

series:

Alexis
Cool as a Cupcake

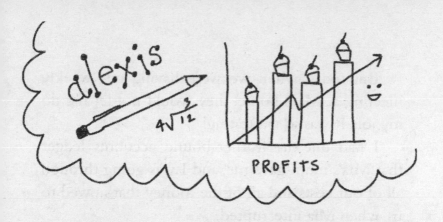

PROFITS

Partners? What Partners?

*B*usiness first. That's one of my mottoes.

When my best friends and I get together to discuss our cupcake company, the Cupcake Club, I am all about business. My name is Alexis Becker, and I am the business planner of the group. This means I kind of take care of everything – pricing, scheduling and ingredient inventory – the nuts and bolts of it all. So when we actually go to make the cupcakes and sell them, we're all set.

Mia Vélaz-Cruz is our fashion-forward, stylish person, who is great at presentation and coming up with really good ideas, and Katie Brown and Emma Taylor are real bakers, so they have lots of ideas on ingredients and how things should taste. Together we make a great team.

But today, when we were having our weekly meeting at Mia's house, they would not let me do my job. It was so frustrating!

I had out the leather-bound accounts ledger that Mia's mum gave me, and I was going through all of our costs and all of the money that's owed to us, when Mia interrupted.

"Ooh! I forgot to tell you I had an idea for your costume for the Homecoming Parade, Katie!" said Mia enthusiastically, as if I wasn't in the middle of reading out columns of numbers for the past two jobs we've had.

The high school in our town has a tradition for their homecoming football game every year. It started when the game fell on Halloween one year, so everyone came in costume. Over the years it's grown into a big costume parade through town, followed by a bonfire rally, and then the game. It's a pretty big deal, and it's happening in about a month, right before Halloween.

"Oh good, what is it?" asked Katie, as if she was thrilled for the interruption.

"Ahem. Are we conducting business here or having a coffee klatch?" That's what our favourite science teacher, Ms Biddle, says when we whisper in class. Apparently, a coffee klatch is something gossipy old ladies do: drink coffee and chatter mindlessly.

"Yeah, c'mon, guys. Let's get through this," said Emma. I know she was trying to be supportive of me, but "get through this"? As if they just had to listen to me before they got to the fun stuff? That was kind of insulting!

"I'm not reading this stuff for my own health, you know," I said. I knew I sounded really huffy, but I didn't care. I do way more behind-the-scenes work than anyone else in this club, and I don't think they have any idea how much time and effort it takes. Now, I *do* love it, but everyone has a limit, and I have almost reached mine.

"Sorry, Alexis! I just was spacing out and it crossed my mind," admitted Mia. It was kind of a lame apology, since she was admitting she was spacing out during my presentation.

"Whatever," I said. "Do you want to listen or should I just forget about it?"

"No, no, we're listening!" protested Katie. "Go on!" But I caught her winking and nodding at Mia as Mia nodded and gestured to her.

I shut the ledger. "Anyway, that's all," I said.

Mia and Katie were so engrossed in their sign language that they didn't even realise I'd cut it short.

Emma seemed relieved and didn't protest.

So that's how it's going to be, I thought. Then fine! I'll just do the books and buy the supplies and do all the scheduling and keep it to myself. No need to involve a whole committee, anyway. I folded my arms across my chest and waited for someone to speak. But of course, it wasn't about business.

"Well?" asked Katie.

"Okay, I was thinking, what about a genie? And you can get George Martinez to be an astronaut. Then you can wear something really dreamy and floaty and magical, like on that old TV show *I Dream of Jeannie* that's on Boomerang?" Mia was smiling in pride at her idea.

"Ooooh! I love that idea!" squealed Katie. "But how do I get George to be a pilot?" She propped her chin on her hand and frowned.

"Wait!" interrupted Emma. "Why would you pick George Martinez to be the pilot?"

Mia looked at her like she was crazy. "Because you have to ask a boy to be your partner for the parade. You know that!"

Emma flushed a deep red. "No, I did not know that. Who told you that?"

I felt a pit growing in my stomach. Even though I was mad and trying to stay out of this annoying conversation, the news stunned me too, and I couldn't remain silent. "Yeah, who told you that?" I added.

Mia and Katie shrugged and looked at each other, then back at us.

"Um, I don't know," said Katie. "It's just common knowledge?"

I found this incredibly annoying since it was our first real homecoming and this is major news. "No, it is *not* common knowledge." I glared at Mia.

"Sorry," said Mia sheepishly.

I pressed my lips together. Then I said, "Well? Who are *you* going with?"

Mia looked away. "I haven't really made up my mind," she said.

"Do you have lots of choices?" I asked. I was half annoyed and half jealous. Mia is really pretty and stylish and not that nervous around boys.

She laughed a little. "Not exactly. But Katie does!"

Emma and I looked at each other, like, *How could we have been so clueless?*

"Stop!" Katie laughed, turning red.

"Well 'fess up! Who are they?" I asked.

Katie rolled her eyes. "Oh, I don't know," she said.

Mia began ticking off names on her fingers. "George Martinez always tortures her in PE, which we all know means he likes her. He even mentioned something about the parade and asked Katie what she was going to be for her costume, right?"

Katie nodded.

Mia continued, "And then there's Joe Fraser. Another possibility."

"Stop!" protested Katie. "That's all. This is too mortifying! Let's change the subject to something boring, like cupcake revenue!"

"Thanks a lot!" I said. I was hurt that she said it because I don't find cupcake revenue boring. I find it fascinating. I love to think of new ways to make money. *How could my best friends and I have such different interests?* I wondered.

"Sorry, but you know what I mean," said Katie. "It stresses me out to talk about who likes who."

Still.

"Well, no one likes me!" said Emma.

"That's not true. I'm sure people like you," said Mia. But I noticed she didn't try to list anyone.

"What do we do if we don't have a boy to go with?" I asked.

"Well, girls could go with their girl friends,

but no one really does that. I think it's just kind of dorky . . ."

I felt a flash of annoyance. Since when was Mia such a know-it-all about homecoming and what was done and what wasn't and what was dorky and what wasn't?

"I guess I could go with Matt . . ." said Emma, kind of thinking out loud.

"What?!" I couldn't contain my surprise. Emma knows I have a crush on her older brother, and in the back of my mind, throughout this whole conversation, I'd been trying to think if I'd have the nerve to ask him. Not that I'd ever ask if he'd do matchy-matchy costumes with me, but just to walk in the parade together. After all, he *had* asked me to dance at my sister's sweet sixteen party.

Emma looked at me. "What?"

I didn't want to admit I'd been thinking that *I'd* ask him, so I said the next thing I could think of. "You'd go with your brother? Isn't *that* kind of dorky?" I felt mean saying it, but I was annoyed.

Emma winced, and I felt a little bad.

But Mia shook her head. "No, not if your brother is older and is cool, like Matt, it's not dorky."

Oh great. Now she'd just given Emma free rein

to ask Matt and I had no one! "You know what? I'm going to check with Dylan on all this," I said. My older sister would certainly know all the details of how this should be done. And she was definitely not dorky.

There was an uncomfortable silence. Finally, I said, "Look, we have a few more weeks to worry about all this, so let's just get back to business, okay?" And at last people were eager to discuss my favourite subject, if only because the other topics had turned out to be so stressful for us.

I cleared my throat and read from my notebook. "We have Jake's best friend Max's party, and Max's mum wants something like what we did for Jake . . ." We'd made Jake Cakes – dirt with worms cupcakes made out of crushed Oreos and gummy worms for Emma's little brother's party, and they were a huge hit.

"Right," said Emma, nodding. "I was thinking maybe we could do Mud Pies?"

"Excellent. Let's think about what we need for the ingredients. There's—"

"Sorry to interrupt, but . . ."

We all looked at Katie.

"Just one more tiny question? Do you think Joe Fraser is a little bit cooler than George Martinez?"

I stared at her coldly. "What does that have to do with Mud Pies?"

"Sorry," said Katie with a shrug. "I was just wondering."

"Anyway, Mud Pie ingredients are . . ."

We brainstormed uninterrupted for another five minutes and got a list of things kind of organised for a Mud Pie proposal and sample baking session. Then we turned to our next big job, baking cupcakes for a regional swim meet fund-raiser.

Mia had been absentmindedly sketching in her notebook, and now she looked up. "I have a great idea for what we could do for the cupcakes for the swim meet!"

"Oh, let's see!" I said, assuming she'd sketched it out. I peeked over her shoulder, expecting to see a cupcake drawing, and instead there was a drawing of a glamorous witch costume, like something out of *Wicked*.

"Oh," I said. Here I'd been thinking we were all engaged in the cupcake topic, and it turned out Mia had been still thinking about the homecoming parade all along.

"Sorry," she said. "But I was *thinking* about cup-cakes."

"Whatever," I said. I tossed my pen down on the table and closed my notebook. "This meeting is adjourned."

"Come on, Alexis," said Mia. "It's not that big a deal."

"Yeah, all work and no play makes for a bad day, boss lady!" added Katie.

"I am *not* the boss lady!" I said. I was mad and hurt. "I don't want to be the boss lady. In fact, I am not any kind of boss. Not anymore! You guys can figure this all out on your own."

I stood up and gathered my things into my bag.

"Hey, Alexis, please! We aren't trying to be mean, we're just distracted!" said Mia.

"You guys think this is all a joke! If I didn't hustle everything along and keep track, nothing would get done!" I said, swinging my bag up over my shoulder. "I feel like I do all the work and then you guys don't even care!"

"Look, it's true you do all the work," agreed Emma. "But we thought you enjoyed it. If you're tired of it, we can divvy it up, right, girls?" she said, looking at Mia and Katie.

"Sure! Why not?" said Mia, flinging her hair behind her shoulders in the way she does when she's getting down to work.

"Fine," I said.

"Look, I'll take on the swim team project, okay?" said Mia.

"And I'll do the Mud Pies," said Emma.

"And I'll do whatever the next big project is," said Katie.

I looked at them all. "What about invoicing, purchasing and inventory?"

The girls each claimed one of the areas, and even though I was torn about giving up my responsibilities, I was glad to see them shouldering some of the work for a change. We agreed that they would e-mail or call me with questions when they needed my help.

"Great," I said. "Now I'm leaving." And I walked home from Mia's quickly, so fast I was almost jogging. My pace was fuelled by anger about the Cupcake Club *and* the desire to get home to my sister, Dylan, as quickly as possible, so I could start asking questions about homecoming and all that it would entail.

Coco Simon always dreamed of opening a cupcake bakery but was afraid she would eat all of the profits. When she's not daydreaming about cupcakes, Coco edits children's books and has written close to one hundred books for children, tweens and young adults, which is a lot less than the number of cupcakes she's eaten. Cupcake Diaries is the first time Coco has mixed her love of cupcakes with writing.

Still Hungry?
There's always room for another Cupcake! Make sure you've read them all!

Katie and the Cupcake Cure
978-0-85707-338-9 £5.99
978-0-85707-402-7 (eBook)

Mia in the Mix
978-0-85707-403-4 £5.99
978-0-85707-404-1 (eBook)

Emma on Thin Icing
978-0-85707-405-8 £5.99
978-0-85707-406-5 (eBook)

Alexis and the Perfect Recipe

978-0-85707-407-2 £5.99

978-0-85707-408-9 (eBook))

Katie, Batter Up!

978-0-85707-883-4 £5.99

978-0-85707-884-1 (eBook)

Mia's Baker's Dozen

978-0-85707-885-8 £5.99

978-0-85707-886-5 (eBook)

Emma All Stirred Up!

978-1-4711-1554-7 £5.99

978-1-4711-1555-4 (eBook)

Alexis Cool As a Cupcake

978-1-4711 1556-1 £5.99

978-1-4711-1557-8 (eBook)

Books 1 & 2 in *The Cupcake Diaries:*

Book 4 in The Cupcake Diaries:

Book 4 in *The Cupcake Diaries*:

The Cupcake Diaries

Alexis
and the
Perfect Recipe

Can your friends and
your crush be the
right party mix?

Coco Simon

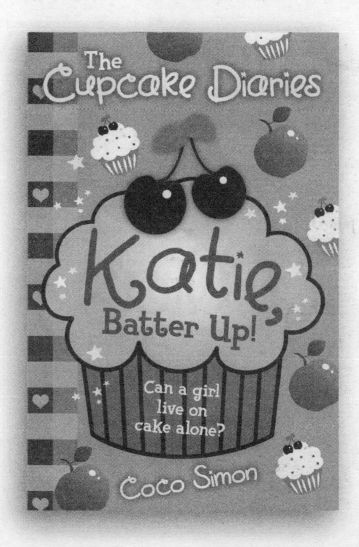

Book 6 in *The Cupcake Diaries*:

The Cupcake Diaries

Mia's
Baker's Dozen

Sometimes there's
just one too many
cupcakes in the mix!

Coco Simon